ISMAT CHUGHTAI (1915–1991) was born in Badayun and is counted among the earliest and foremost women Urdu writers. She focused on women's issues with a directness and intensity unparalleled in Indian literature among writers of her generation. She is the author of several collections of short stories, novellas, a novel, *Terhi Lakir* (The Crooked Line), a collection of reminiscences and essays, *My Friend, My Enemy*, and a memoir, *Kaghazi Hai Perahan* (The Paper-thin Garment). With her husband, Shahid Latif, a film director, she produced and co-directed six Hindustani films, and produced a further six, independently, after his death.

TAHIRA NAQVI, a translator of Urdu fiction and prose, taught English for twenty years, has taught Urdu at Columbia, and now heads the Urdu programme at New York University. She has translated Ismat Chughtai's short stories, her novel and her essays. She has also translated the works of Khadija Mastur, Sa'dat Hasan Manto and Munshi Premchand. Naqvi also writes fiction in English. She has published two collections of short fiction, *Attar of Roses and Other Stories of Pakistan* and *Dying in a Strange Country*. Her short stories have been widely anthologized.

Obsession
&
Wild Pigeons

ISMAT CHUGHTAI

women
UNLIMITED
an associate of
kali for women

SPEAKING
TIGER

WOMEN UNLIMITED
(an associate of Kali for Women)
7/10, Sarvapriya Vihar, First Floor
New Delhi – 110016, India

SPEAKING TIGER PUBLISHING PVT. LTD
4381/4, Ansari Road, Daryaganj
New Delhi – 110002

Obsession and *Wild Pigeons* were first published in English
in India as part of *A Chughtai Quartet* by Women Unlimited,
an associate of Kali for Women, 2014
This edition jointly published in paperback by Speaking Tiger and
Women Unlimited 2019

Urdu original copyright © heirs of Ismat Chughtai
This translation copyright © Tahira Naqvi

ISBN: 978-93-88326-97-1
eISBN: 978-93-88326-51-3

10 9 8 7 6 5 4 3 2 1

Typeset in Adobe Caslon Pro by Jojy Philip

Obsession
(*Saudai*)

Buzdil, *the film starring Kishore Sahu, Premnath and Nimmi, produced and directed by Ismat's husband Shahid Latif, is the basis for this novel.*

1

Chandar slid down the banister and landed on the floor with a loud thud. As always, Masi's heart lurched.

"You wretch, if you miss your step you'll break your bones," she said, striking her forehead. But Chandar didn't listen. He slithered down like a turtle every day and every day Masi's heart took a plunge.

"You troublemaker, one day you'll fall on your face and all your teeth will break and get stuck in your throat! Nobody listens to me, what am I to do?"

Chandar curled his upper lip until it was touching his nose, then with a hissing sound he swooped down on the dining table.

He loved teasing Masi. He had also made Pimo's life miserable. She was a year and a half younger than Chandar, but she regarded him as her guru. And what choice did she have? He dragged her by her tiny braids, tripped her again and again with his foot, pounded her dolls and ordered her to obey his every command.

"Hold your nose and say salaam to me seven times."

"Walk on one leg and fetch me a glass of water! And I will not speak to you ever again if you spill a single drop."

Not speaking meant that he would give her a wallop every time he passed her and jostle her with his elbow, or pinch her nose. Experience had taught her that she couldn't win with Chandar. The only person he was afraid of was Barre Bhaiya. He regarded him as the world's greatest, most esteemed and most brilliant human being. Barre Bhaiya was a full fifteen years older than him and was so virtuous, so superior that it was impossible to utter one word against him.

That's why his name was Suraj. And when the rays of the sun fall on the moon only then does the moon begin to shine. If the Sun God was driven to anger, the face of Chandra would turn black like soot.

That was why Masi performed aarti before Suraj every morning and evening, because he was a god, and that's why she called Chandar a demon. Suraj had never beaten anybody or teased anyone, nor had he ever lied or stolen, and he had never played gulli danda or kabbadi with the boys on the street. His mother knew that there was not a single boy in the neighbourhood fit to socialise with Suraj. His companions were not people, they were princes and sadhus and other holy men who existed in fairy tales and fables.

Masi always sang Suraj's praises. It was common knowledge that she had decided he would marry her daughter, Usha, and that was why she toiled ceaselessly to mould him into the best of all sons-in-law. Constant praise had made him think so highly of himself that even if he wanted to indulge in any mischief, he would worry about losing his reputation, afraid that he would be regarded as an ordinary human being and cease to have praise piled on him. Masi would no longer perform aartis, Chandar and Pimo would stop being terrified of him, and then what would be left in the world for him? At this young age, respect was the only thing he possessed. He wasn't going to let anyone steal his treasure.

On her deathbed Mataji had held Pimo's and Chandar's hands and said to Suraj, "My son, you are now both father and mother to them, don't do anything that will make them stray from the right path. If the honour of the family is tarnished, my soul will never find peace."

Pitaji had passed away a year before that. He had rejected the rules of the world and lost everything after becoming involved with a woman of loose morals. Then he quarrelled with her, got drunk and was killed in a road accident.

Masi was a dear friend of Mataji. Her husband had also abandoned her and the two unhappy friends constantly poured homilies into Suraj's ears about virtuous living.

Masi was of the opinion that Suraj's father, Tarbhun Nathji, had not been raised properly. To begin with, his parents had loosened their reins, then he was married to a woman who lacked spirit and could never really control him which was why he had died young. For fifteen years Suraj was the only and most beloved child. Fearing her husband's lack of attention, the mother dug her claws into her son. Then fortune smiled on her and she had two more children, but neither received the same love as Suraj. Chandar and Pimo were raised by the servants.

Sermons were not considered enough to keep Suraj from going astray, so Maa had Suraj betrothed to Usha Rani and both she and Masi embarked on a campaign to nurture a blessed union. But before they could arrange the wedding, death overtook her.

When Maa died, Pimo was a year-and-a-half, Chandar was three and Suraj had just completed his eighteenth year. Burdened with such immense responsibility at such a young age, Suraj began to mature before his time. He had never been naughty, but now he became a complete sadhu. Afraid that he might fall into bad company in school, he was tutored at home. Maa had been dead for three years now, but not a day went by when Masi didn't tearfully recount the events surrounding her passing. Several times during the day she would repeat Maa's sayings. Chandar and Pimo had forgotten Maa, but Suraj felt her influence still and was also weighed down by Masi's authority.

Along with supervising Suraj, Masi kept a vigilant eye on Usha as well. She was to be the queen of the house some day, destined to be Suraj's Yogiya. Masi kept her busy with studying and embroidering. Someone who has been burnt by boiling milk learns to fear even the froth on the surface of buttermilk. Men are like monkeys; no matter how much you train them, teach them, the minute they get an opportunity they will climb back up a tree. And she wanted to teach Usha special tactics so that her husband would not be able to climb the tree, would stay on the straight and narrow. Compared to her mother, Usha was like a cow, she went in whichever direction her mother steered her.

Masi was not a dishonest person. She nursed her love for her friend with great dedication. Looked after her during her illness more diligently than a sister would. Even though she was mistress of everything in the house, she took nothing for herself. She did the work of four servants. Actually, the affairs of the bank and management of the estate were handled by Sitaramji. He was a very gracious, honest man who had devoted his life to religious exercise, austerity and celibacy, and was raising these three children as his own. But the rest of the belongings in the house and all the jewellery were in Masi's charge. Except for the jewellery the dying woman had placed in Masi's hands, there wasn't a single strand she had touched—what need did she have to, anyway? Maa had left all the jewellery for Suraj's wife. When Chandar and Suraj grew up she would see to their needs, why worry now? Suraj would handle everything. Who else besides Usha was Suraj's bride! Why did Masi need anything?

From a very young age Usha had begun to regard Suraj as the god of her heart. Ever since she was twelve or thirteen she had been taking care of Suraj's needs like a good wife. Without waiting for instructions from Masi, she would get hot water readied for his bath, supervise his change of clothing, and at mealtimes, arrange delicious morsels of food in his tray. Without his saying a word she would know whether he needed salt, a hot chilli or a glass of water. She embroidered chikan kurtas for him, knitted new styles of sweaters, and embroidered bouquets on his handkerchiefs.

It was her house after all; if something broke or was misplaced she scolded the servants just as the mistress of the house would.

By now Suraj had become used to being waited upon by her and regarding her as his, never questioning the attention she showered on him. But unlike other young men, he never teased her or looked at her amorously.

"He doesn't like behaving irresponsibly, he's not a vagabond, nor is my daughter a girl without morals," declared Masi. And if someone pointed to Suraj's lack of feeling towards Usha she would brush it off, saying, "Why, he's just like his mother."

It was Chandar who took after his father: restless and stubborn. It really didn't matter if he suffered an ill fate. Satwanti's womb wouldn't have been damageed if he hadn't been born—Suraj, equal to a hundred children, was present, wasn't he? When the time came everything would be taken care of. Masi was confident of her ability to keep things in order, and she was aware that, if and when the need arose, she would be able to teach Usha the art of ensnaring her man. As a matter of fact she was already doing her best.

"My child, even Bhagwan, when you serve him, will look kindly on you, and Suraj is just a man."

Masi herself had never truly waited on her own husband. That poor man was not her match anyway. Even if he had been a police inspector or a deputy instead of a clerk, he wouldn't have been able to save himself from her clutches; she would have outshone Sati-Savitri as the dutiful wife.

As was his custom, Chandar jumped over the furniture and attacked the dining table.

"Hai, hai, Chandar!"

"What is it, Masi?"

"Where are you sitting?"

"On the chair, Masi."

"Arre, whose chair are you sitting on?"

"Oh, on Barre Bhaiya's." Chandar leapt up as if he had tainted a god's throne in a temple, and plonked himself on the chair next to it.

Masi looked respectfully in the direction of the staircase from where the Sun God was about to descend.

"Stop, Chandar!" Masi admonished when she saw him reaching for the fruit. "Wait for Barre Sarkar, you good-for-nothing. How greedy you are!"

Stand at attention, ready to pay your respects!

Mahabali approaches.

The atmosphere was imbued with the power of his presence. Receiving a signal from her mother, Usha quickly jumped up and, pulling her dupatta over her head, stationed herself like a puppet at the bottom of the stairs. First the sound of footsteps was heard on the stairs, then the Sun God raised his head in the east.

Big, deep set eyes, thick wavy hair of which a lock trembled on the forehead, a sharp nose. Dressed in a foamy white dhoti, a loose kurta of heavy silk, a brown pashmina shawl draped on his shoulders, he made a radiant appearance at the top of the stairs. (He had borrowed this mode of dress from the Bengalis.) Then, with measured steps he came down the stairs.

"Namaskar," Usha's soft voice rustled.

"Namaskar." He looked past her in the distance and joined his palms together, brushing the lock of hair on his forehead with his hand as he did so.

"May you live long, my precious son, may you live a thousand years!" Masi rushed towards him to ward off the evil eye, but he cleverly evaded her grasp for fear that she might disturb the lock of hair which he had arranged carefully, standing before the mirror for a long time, but which gave the impression of having carelessly fallen over his forehead.

Every morning it was this very lock that Masi threatened to fix and this really made him angry. But he never allowed his anger to show because gods don't get angry.

Chandar was starving. As soon as Barre Sarkar sat down he pounced on the food.

Which was when Pimo hopped in, made a face at Chandar and dropped into a chair.

"Pimo Rani."

"Ji?"

"What did you forget to do today?"

"Uhh…"

"All right, say namaskar first," Masi ordered and Pimo immediately put her palms together and like Chandar, proceeded to stuff her mouth with food.

Masi quickly picked up the plate of ladoos and placed it in front of Suraj.

"Let Barre Bhaiya eat first. My dear boy, I'll bring some fresh pooris for you. I don't trust the servants, I'll make them myself. Actually, Usha is the one who makes them every morning. Here, girl, peel a pomegranate for Sarkar."

Keeping in mind the future relationship between them she discouraged Usha from calling him Barre Bhaiya.

"But why do you have to bother? Have all the servants died?"

"Arre, my son, what bother? Hai, how much you think of me! My dearest child, if your Sati Savitri mother had not taken care of me, where would we be now?" Masi immediately began sniffling. Her weeping always amused Pimo and Chandar and they burst out laughing.

"Here, have an orange," Masi said when she saw Chandar reaching for one. Her tears had disappeared.

"No, he'll cough at night." Suraj pushed Chandar's hand away.

It amused Barre Sarkar to see her change gears like this, and he would quickly place a handkerchief on his nose that would begin to twitch in anticipation of the laughter that threatened to erupt. How could he possibly laugh?

Masi left to fetch fresh pooris, Usha bent down to tie Pimo's shoelaces while Pimo fed Tommy biscuits under the table. For one moment it was all clear. There were fresh, fragrant ladoos on the table. The child hiding in Barre Sarkar's heart leapt out and he snatched up two ladoos in a flash. Just then he heard Masi's footsteps—no time to pop them into his mouth and not possible to put them back on the plate, so he deposited them in his pocket.

"Hai, Chandar!" Seeing that some ladoos were missing Masi began beating her chest. "Why, you scoundrel! The doctor has forbidden you to eat sweets and you gulped down not one but two ladoos!"

"I didn't eat a single one!" Chandar protested.

"And now you're lying, you bad boy! Show me your hands."

Chandar shoved his hands under Masi's nose. She recoiled.

"Open your mouth."

After a thorough search she concluded that he had swallowed the ladoos without chewing them first. She grabbed his ear.

"That's enough, Masi, he made a mistake. Forgive him, he won't do it again," Barre Sarkar said.

"I'm being blamed for nothing, Masi, I didn't take the ladoos."

"Then Pimo must have eaten them." Barre Sarkar glared at Pimo.

"No, Barre Bhaiya, I didn't. Ask Usha Didi."

"Usha Rani certainly didn't eat them, so where did they go?" Barre

Sarkar turned his large black eyes towards Chandar and glowered at him. Fearfully, Chandar lowered his eyes.

"You see? You see how guilty he looks, the wretch! Here my son, eat." Masi pushed the plate of ladoos towards Suraj.

"No, Masi, you know I don't like sweets," Suraj said, lovingly caressing the ladoos in his pocket. "Chandar, if you do something so inexcusable again—well, I won't tolerate it."

Chandar and Pimo exchanged knowing glances and quickly slipped away. Masi and Usha brought out the ledger containing the daily accounts.

"Pudina, three annas, lauki four annas…tori…" Masi rendered an account of every little item in order to impress Barre Sarkar so that he would see how profitable this relationship with her and Usha was. But Barre Sarkar only wanted to claw her face.

"Ginger, one and a half pao…garam masala—"

"Oh…" Barre Sarkar suddenly and dramatically seized his head with his hands. Masi jumped up.

"Ai hai, my child, what's the matter?"

"Headache…I have a headache."

"Arri, Usha, don't stand there like—tell Munshiji—"

"No, don't send for the doctor. Get my pills from my drawer."

"Go, you silly girl," she pushed Usha out and quickly began to fan him with a corner of her sari.

"Wa…ter," Barre Sarkar said, tossing his head. Masi ran to get a glass while he calmly retrieved a ladoo from his pocket and dropped it into his mouth. Closing his eyes, he began chewing it with pleasure.

When Masi returned with a glass of water, panting and out of breath, and Usha arrived with the bottle of pills, he gave them a startled look as if he didn't know who they were.

"Your headache…pills…water," Masi reminded him.

"Water? Pills? Oh, I see. No need any more."

And he turned casually to the paper. Both mother and daughter were left baffled by his behaviour and were sorry that they had lost an opportunity to serve.

Barre Sarkar took great pleasure in frequently tricking them like this. He was so clever that he could hoodwink anyone and then, remembering what he had done, would laugh heartily and feel very pleased with himself.

2

"It's true. If you dig a hole with your finger a dwarf will come out of the earth." Chandar made up a story.

"Hey, Ram! Then he'll play with me, Chot Bhaiya?"

Pimo had barely scratched an inch of earth with her tiny finger when her nails, filled with dirt, began to hurt.

"Chot Bhaiyaji."

"What?"

"Have you ever seen a fairy?"

"Many times."

"Oh, you haven't, you liar."

"It's true, I swear."

"Well then, show me too."

"You're a fool, you won't be able to see a fairy."

"Why?"

"Because I said so."

"Chot Bhaiya."

"What?"

"My finger hurts."

"I told you, didn't I, that you wouldn't be able to dig a hole."

"Unhuh...fairy, Bhaiyaji."

"All right, look over there."

"Where?" Scared, she edged closer to him.

"There...there...on the pomegranate tree. See it?"

"Ohh, that's just a pifon."

"Not a pifon silly, a pigeon. In reality it's a fairy."

"A fairy? How do you know?"

"Well, I just know, that's all. It's a fairy. Be very still and you'll see that the bird will flip around and turn into a fairy." But unfortunately Pimo sneezed just then and the pigeon flew away.

"You see, you silly girl! Why did you have to sneeze? If she had become angry she would have waved her wand and turned you into a mouse."

"The fairy?"

"Yes."

"She turns people into mice if she gets angry?"

"Of course."

"Chot Bhaiya."

"Yes."

"Let's go home, I'm scared." Pimo began whimpering. "I don't want to see any fairies."

But Chandar was staring at the pile of leaves next to the tree. There was a tiny pink hand lying among the leaves.

"A hand!" Chandar darted across but Pimo stumbled and fell and started bawling. Chandar stopped to help her up and his fear diminished. Mistaking it for a flower, a butterfly had alighted on the hand.

"Look, Pimo," Chandar said, grabbing her.

"A hand? Who left it here?"

"Definitely a fairy. Left it here by mistake," Chandar said.

"Where is the fairy?"

"She flew away."

"But left her hand here?"

"That's what it looks like. She forgot it. Pick it up, Pimo."

"No, Chot Bhaiya, let's go home." Pimo was terrified.

"Arre, don't be afraid, you fool. Wait, let's see."

Chandar picked up a twig and cautiously touched the hand. A tiny finger moved and with a loud croak a wild duck suddenly flapped out of the pile of leaves. Terrified, they both fled, but Chandar bravely returned and moved the leaves with a stick. Brown curly hair and a fair-complexioned face emerged, and a pair of large, frightened eyes opened. Tiny lips quivered. A two or two-and-a-half year old girl, dressed in rags, rose to her feet, brushing off leaves from her body as she did so. The two children froze.

"You're a fairy, aren't you?" Chandar asked apprehensively.

The girl nodded.

"You see!" Chandar turned to Pimo triumphantly.

"Where are your wings?" Pimo asked, emboldened.

The girl looked around her timidly and then began to whimper.

"You fool, now see what you've done, you made her cry. Here, fairy, do you want a toffee?"

The girl shook her head.

"Oh, the poor thing is hungry." Pimo's eyes brimmed with tears. "She doesn't have wings, Chot Bhaiya, how will she fly?"

"Don't cry, the poor thing has lost her wings, but new wings will sprout."

"Don't cry, fairy."

"What should we do now?"

"Let's take her home. Fairy, will you come with us?"

The girl shook her head again but the two children dragged her with them. Rani, the potter's wife, started screaming when they returned.

"Hai, Masiji, Chote Bhaiya has brought home some girl!"

"Girl? Have you lost your mind? It must be one of the milkman's daughters, get her out of here, the wretch."

"Ai ji, they won't let me throw her out, they're hitting me, the two of them."

"Arre, which two?"

"Ai ji, Bua, it's Chote Bhaiya and Pimo. Let them be, Masi, tell the police and they'll come and take her away."

But the children set up a real commotion. Clung to Suraj's feet and started weeping.

Masi ground her teeth and said, "Well, I'll see how Chandar stops Thanedar Sahib!"

"We'll beat up the police, too!" Chandar declared, waving his hockey stick in the air. Like a brave knight he was bent on protecting the fairy.

"You'll be handcuffed, my boy."

"We'll break the handcuffs!"

But when the police arrived and made inquiries they discovered that the girl didn't belong to anyone in the village. Who knows who had abandoned her in the woods.

"She must be illegitimate," Masi decided, "take her to the orphanage."

"Let her stay here until we find someone who claims her," Barre Sarkar said, "and when the children get tired of her she can be sent off to the orphanage."

But the girl was indeed a fairy. No one came to claim her and she continued to live at the house. Usha Rani was still playing with dolls so she cut up old clothes and stitched shiny garments for her. For a few days she slept with Rani, the potter's wife, in the small room next to the kitchen, and then started sleeping on the floor in the children's room. A few nice words to Didi, and the children were able to have new clothes made for her. Sometimes Masi would get upset and exclaim, "Who knows whether the wretch is a bhangi's child or a chamar's offspring, eating at our table with us." But the girl not only gained Chandar and Pimo's devotion, Usha Rani too had become very fond of her. And so the children's demands continued to be met. Suraj did not object to her presence, but she was terrified of him and ran to hide in some corner the moment she saw him. Or she would seek refuge behind Chandar or Pimo, or bury her face in Usha's dupatta. If she was crying and he appeared, she would be stunned into silence, and if she was laughing she would clamp her hand on her mouth. When Barre Sarkar saw the overwhelming effect he had on her he swelled with pride.

Usha dressed her up in beautiful clothes as if she were a little she-monkey and named her Chandni. Chandar's Chandni. After all it was Chandar who had found her.

Chandar and Pimo were crazy about her. Sometimes they would pass their fingers over her shoulders gingerly to see if she had sprouted wings—she might fly away if she had!

Despite Masi's opposition she continued to receive an education because she was always with the children.

"I don't know why my heart is filled with fear," Masi would heave a long sigh and say. "It's not a good omen that rubbish from the wayside should fill one's eyes. Who knows what trouble this girl will be when she grows up."

Barre Sarkar was a person of superior qualities so it was just him and his books of philosophy. The only time he left the house was to ride or swim. The estate was large. The canal was theirs, the woods were theirs as well, and the lake, too. If only Chandar had been closer to him in age he wouldn't feel so terribly lonely. How close Chandar and Pimo were. Sometimes he felt such an urge to laugh loudly like them, climb trees and run about, but his overly mature self came in the way of all that.

He never quite understood Usha. Bashful, she seemed to have no other use except to steal furtive looks at him. The thoughts that arose in his mind when he saw her growing up scared him because he thought they were dirty. He began to be annoyed by her presence. Chandar was such a fool. Didn't like studying, was naughty and harassed everyone, especially Masi who couldn't handle him at all. She was convinced he would grow up to be a bandit, and given half a chance would squander the family's wealth.

One day the children were playing ball in the garden. Chandar was beating the girls at the game and suddenly the ball slipped from Chandni's hands and landed close to Suraj's feet. He picked it up quietly and slipped it into his pocket. When the children came looking for it he pretended he was reading the newspaper. As the children looked in the bushes for the ball, the dormant youth in Suraj suddenly awakened. He took the ball from his pocket and gazed longingly at it. He looked around, then threw the ball in the air and kicked it hard when it came down. The ball went flying through Masi's window, shattered it, and hit Masi's head hard. Masi had been deeply engrossed in reading aloud from the Gita. When the ball hit her she let out a shriek, glared wrathfully at the ball, then marched into the garden, screaming and yelling. Chandar was still searching. Masi grabbed his ear and dragged him towards Barre Sarkar. Chandni saw Chandar being mistreated, suspended herself from Masi's wrist and dug her tiny pointed teeth into her.

"Punish me, but leave her alone," Pimo begged and took the entire force of Masi's pounding on her own back. Suraj was watching all this and couldn't help laughing at Masi's foolishness. When the case was presented in his court he pretended to be engrossed in his paper. Masi felt a surge of love for him.

"So Chandar, you've become very naughty," he scolded Chandar. The Suraj who couldn't resist a ball a little while earlier had disappeared; the Barre Sarkar who was like a god remained. He was afraid to admit that both these beings were actually the same. The despicable Suraj was not Barre Sarkar, he was someone else; if he could hide after committing an offence, he had nothing in common with his other self.

"Barre Bhaiya, I'm telling the truth, I didn't throw the ball," Chandar stammered.

"And now you're lying. Come on, ask for Masi's forgiveness."

"Forgive me, Masi." Chandar laid down his weapons and Masi accepted his apology.

3

Moments flowed into each other to become years. The tiny jamun plant that Chandar and Pimo had planted on the banks of the lake now swayed like a massive tree. Suraj's authority also grew like a giant and permeated the entire household. The children respected him more than they would their own parents. Chandar was still afraid of looking him in the eye. Pimo was favoured because she was young, but she too didn't have the courage to talk back to him. The darkest shadow lay on Usha Rani's heart and mind. The giant had incapacitated her completely. She was ruled by Barre Sarkar. She circled mechanically around the Sun God. Gave him breakfast, uncovered the bread basket for him, sprinkled the right amount of salt and pepper on his eggs, buttered his toast, then cleared the dishes herself. There was neither joy nor discomfort in this service anymore.

She is Barre Sarkar's fiancee and this is what the fates have decreed for her. There was only one man in the world for her and that was Suraj. One day she would be married to him, Barre Sarkar would lift her veil.

Munshiji had come to this house as a teacher for the children. He had wasted his youth waiting for Usha Rani's love. What could he do except see her and sigh soulfully? If she appeared while he was tutoring the children, he would flounder helplessly. Usha loved making him uncomfortable, would deliberately laugh sweetly and say things to tease him.

"Munshiji, if someone falls madly in love with you, what will you do?"

"I…I…well…" Munshiji would break out in a sweat.

"I mean anyone…for example, if a girl is loved by a very special man, what should she do?"

"Should she say without any hesitation that she loves him?"

"Yes…yes…if."

"Why if? She's a girl from a high caste, not some low class, dimwitted girl, and he too is of a good caste, very talented and handsome."

"Oh?" Munshiji began to feel the conversation was not about him.

"But he never says anything." Usha Rani would then look sad. "Perhaps because it's not proper to do so. Is that true, Munshiji?"

"Yes…yes, I think so…" Munshiji would become more dejected.

"That's why she worships him, considers him her guru, considers making a life for herself at his feet, but he doesn't know this and that's why he says nothing. This is what it is, isn't it, Munshiji?"

And Munshiji would see the fate of his love revealed to him clearly. Usha Rani's beauty and youth were a punishment for him. He had no relatives who would arrange his marriage somewhere else so that he could forget her. He would pass his life as an unhappy rejected lover and burn like a cinder. If a drop of water keeps falling in one place, it creates a dent even in a stone. His suffering on account of his love for Usha had created many a dent in his heart and he had grown accustomed to this pain, but of late his passion had begun to develop a bitter taste.

Once in a while Barre Sarkar became irritated with Usha and scolded her, and then he would give her some false hope in order to assuage his remorse. Smile at her, and flowers would bloom in Usha Rani's heart.

Masi would try to advise her. "My child, why do you allow these irrational thoughts to trouble you? If he didn't like you, why would he feel obliged? Wouldn't he have asked to marry someone else?"

Sometimes Masi lost her patience. Was there something missing in Usha that she didn't appeal to Barre Sarkar? She insisted that Usha Rani dress well, wear the latest fashions, and she herself kept her close to Suraj on one pretext or another.

But Masi had been right in saying that Chandni would grow up and make trouble. When she reached womanhood she was like a fragrant flower in full bloom. Such vivacity could not exist in a girl from a respectable family. She must be the child of a harlot.

Chandni was so confident of her beauty that she became fearless. She even stopped being afraid of Barre Sarkar. The moment he arrived on the scene everyone fell silent, but she would continue to chatter.

"Why should I be quiet? I wasn't swearing. Arre, you're afraid of him for no reason. I'm not. When he glared at me yesterday with his big eyes he thought, this wretch will die of fright!"

"Hai, O mother, Barre Bhaiya glared at you?"

"Yes."

"Then?"

"Then what? I made a face at him," Chandni laughed.

"You're lying!"

"I swear."

"And then?"

"Then what? I ran off."

"And what if Masi had seen you?"

"Arre, who's afraid of Masi? She just barks, she can't bite!"

"All right, so if you aren't afraid of him why do you call him Barre Sarkar?"

"What else shall I call him?"

"Why don't you call him Barre Bhaiya?"

"Oh, stop it."

"Why?"

"Rani teases me. Is he your brother-in-law already that you call him Barre Bhaiya, she says. That's why I'm shy."

"But one day you'll have to call him Barre Bhaiya."

"Stop, or I'll hit you," Chandni said, acting coy.

Chandni was extremely impish. She enjoyed being a tomboy. Masi's cobra-like head would be raised in vigilance, making sure no girl and boy became too free with each other, although she did send Usha to Barre Sarkar's room again and again. Maybe, if something happened, a marriage would become inevitable. But Barre Sarkar was made of stone. Masi was afraid that Chandni might ensnare Chandar in her net, but she was quite sure she didn't have the power to rid Chandar of the love and awe he had for Barre Sarkar. Even now one look from him would make Chandar weak in the knees. He might be good for nothing, but he was ready to sacrifice his life for his older brother. Then it occurred to her that if he blackened his name through his association with the girl, he would no longer have the courage to ask for his inheritance.

But Chandni's feistiness came to an end the day she became suspicious of Barre Sarkar's intentions. If it had been some other girl she wouldn't have given it another thought. But because she had no inhibitions herself she immediately understood. Chandni was bathing and suddenly a sixth sense told her that someone was peeking at her. She had taken off her clothes, had already put some herbal soap in her hair when she felt there was someone at the window that opened onto the lawn. That witch, the washerman's daughter, she's a wicked one, always sneaking around. Chandni quickly draped a towel around her. A glance at the shadow on the glass pane of the door established that it wasn't a child. The shadow moved, the dark spot on the polished glass was erased and light shone through. It was not a dark spot. Someone had scraped off the polish on the glass in order to look through it. It was the gaze of a person with a filthy mind, someone who had run away when she was alerted to his presence. Humiliation and shame made it difficult for her to continue bathing.

She asked Usha to cover up the spot the next day, but a few days later she found a pea-sized hole scratched out on the other pane. She started bathing in Usha's bathroom, but Masi made such a fuss that she stopped.

Chandni decided that she would somehow catch this person who had been peeping through the hole. She went in one day and started to run the water. She unlatched the bolt on the door opening onto the garden and fixed her eyes on the glass pane. Whoever peered in wouldn't know that a light shadow could be seen from the inside. The moment an eye appeared at the scratched spot Chandni opened the door wide. Barre Sarkar was standing in front of her and his eyes were filled with all the filth of the world. She was transfixed. Then she fled to her room and fell on her bed like a wounded bird.

She couldn't believe her eyes. It was as if she had seen Bhagwan devouring cow-dung. If she mentioned this to anyone, a storm would break and she wouldn't be able to stay in this house for another minute. So all she did was to tell Pimo that the glass panes should be covered with paper so no one could look in. From that day on Chandni avoided Barre Sarkar. Leave alone looking him in the eye, she wouldn't even glance in his direction. It was the worst at dinner time—she sat cowering like a mouse between Pimo and Chandar and after quickly swallowing a few mouthfuls of food, she would dash off from the dining room.

For several days after this incident Barre Sarkar remained confined to his room. He didn't eat, didn't change his clothes. All night he smoked one cigarette after another and paced about restlessly. He abused this wretched Suraj who had behaved so dishonourably. He would strangle him if he could. He didn't want to see anyone. Masi and everyone else in the house was completely surprised.

Everyone except Chandni knocked on his door, but he told them off. After several days of atonement, and when he was sure that Chandni had not said a word to anyone, he felt somewhat encouraged. Soon he reassured himself that there was no way Chandni knew what his crime was. He had just been standing near the door, what was so bad about that? This was his house, he was the master, there could be a thousand reasons for his presence there. Chandni would never muster enough courage to misconstrue his intentions. After confidently arriving at this conclusion, he emerged from his room. That very day Masi had tied a ribbon on the trellised grate of Sarna Devi's shrine and made a vow. Seeing the arrow hit its mark she immediately fell at the Devi's feet.

"Oh, my son, I have been so worried. What is the matter?"

"Nothing at all, Masi. I wasn't feeling very well and thought I should fast for a few days. All of you start worrying for no reason at all. I also had to look through a few books on philosophy to write up some notes."

Chandni disappeared the moment he came out of his room. After this it became routine—the moment the sun came out the moon's light was extinguished. The matter was soon forgotten, but the chase of the lion and the doe had begun. The doe sprinted away the instant she smelled the lion's presence.

Often at night Chandni would have a nightmare and would start sobbing, felt as if she had landed on a heap of dry leaves somewhere far away, in a desolate forest, completely alone, surrounded by a frightening silence. There was no one around, no one. She was running, two eyes emerged from their sockets and crawled towards her, making her stumble! Long serpentine eyes entangled her entire body, a strange fear slowly grounded her. She couldn't breathe, her lungs had collapsed, she would keep falling like this, one lifetime after another. She would wake with a start, draw a deep breath and begin weeping, stifling her sobs so that she wouldn't wake Pimo who was asleep next to her.

Where was she born? Did she have a mother? A father? If yes, then why had she been abandoned? Perhaps a fairy had dropped her on earth and then forgotten all about her.

Every single particle of her being was trapped in the bonds of the Thakur family. Indeed they had picked her up from the dirt and turned her into a princess. And Chandar—how can there be moonlight without the moon? How sad and dark the world would be without a moon. She was Chandar's shadow, wasn't she? She had longed to be part of him ever since she was a little girl. How accepting his love was! And she was his…he had found her, hadn't he?

Pimo! Who knows what good deeds Chandni had performed in her previous life to get a friend like Pimo as a reward in this one. Pimo's friendship, her sisterly love, her maternal affection, call it what you like, it was her life's most beautiful gift. Pimo was not a human being, she was the avatar of some goddess who always protected her.

And she couldn't say enough about Usha Didi. She's Usha Didi, isn't she, the queen of the household. No one can find fault with her. She's loving towards everyone, takes care of them all. Her heart is filled with love, isn't it? But her god is a real slab of stone, doesn't lift his gaze to see that the devotee is a flesh and blood creature not a mound of sandy soil! She doesn't ask for anything. The fire in her heart lit, her forehead touching the ground in worship, she sits waiting, waiting for her god's eye to open, and then the flame of her love will ignite his heart, and her life will be fulfilled.

Her palms pressed together, Chandni pleads with Bhagwan, "Hey, Bhagwan, when will you yield? When will Usha Devi find happiness? How long will the little bird wait to slake her thirst?"

But Masi just barks, she doesn't bite. Her husband died when she was young and ever since she has devoted her life to Usha, determined to serve the entire household in the hope that one day she will be the queen of this house. She wasn't interested in food or clothes; all she ever wished was that Usha's destiny would awaken one day. Was this wish so complicated that Bhagwan was having a hard time fulfilling it? This troublesome situation is all due to the fact that Bhagwan does not accept this offering. O you who nurture us, your godliness will not be marred if you fill his heart with Usha's love.

One day she attempted to casually broach the subject with Chandar.

"Chandarji?"

"Hunh."

"What will you do if Chandni dies one day?"

"The moon has to drown before the moonlight can die. Are you scolding me?" Chandar looked at her through halfshut eyes.

"Hai, curse my mouth, why would I scold you? But you know, life is uncertain, people do die."

"Stop it, you silly girl. Why all this talk about death at this time?"

Chandni sighed deeply and placed her cheek on his palm. "Well, what if someone snatches me from you?"

"No one can snatch you from me. I'll shoot him."

"Your Bhaiya can't snatch me either?"

Suddenly Chandar pushed her away violently and stood up. His eyes blazed. "How dare you mention Bhaiya's name?"

"Chandro—" Chandni let go of his hand in fear.

"You wretch, he's like my father!" Chandar said in a voice choked with terror.

"I made a mistake, Chandar, I spoke without thinking, I didn't really mean it."

"I'll smash your face in if you say something like this again! He loves me so much, and who do you think you are, you bhangan?"

"I'm the dirt at your feet, Chandar—your shadow." She edged towards him.

"Get away from me, I'm very angry. You insulted Bhaiya."

"Then beat me, Chandar—slap me hard," Chandni said, her eyes filling with tears.

"All right, enough." Chandar softened.

"I just said it without thinking. He's my master also, just as he is yours. What I meant was—if he turns me out of the house and…" Chandni tried to change her position.

"Then I'll leave the house as well, but that will never happen. Bhaiya is so good, never in his life has he refused me anything."

"But who knows anything about me—who knows who I am, and you're the son of a Thakur."

"You're Chandni and I don't know anything more than that." Chandar took her into his arms and squeezed her so hard she could hardly breathe, and they both rolled on the cool grass. Chandni grabbed Chandar's hair to steady herself but trembled when she realised that she seemed to be losing herself in him.

Suddenly there was a rustling in the dry leaves and the two of them drew apart hastily. They glimpsed Barre Sarkar with a gun in his hands, casually gazing at the sky. Chandni quickly hid herself behind the trunk of a tree. Barre Sarkar glared at Chandar who, looking guilty, was still sprawled on the grass. There were serpents glinting in Barre Sarkar's eyes. Chandar got up quickly and brushed off the grass from his clothes.

All of a sudden Barre Sarkar broke into a smile and said gently, "You're lying on the wet grass, you'll catch a chill. Go inside and put on a sweater."

"Yes, yes, Bhaiya," Chandar said, trying to escape.

"Are you studying for your exams?"

"Yes, Bhaiya."

"This is a nice place for studying, but where are your books?"

"Err…they're…in my room."

"Well, that's all right. But as a matter of principle, you should be sleeping in your room and not here."

"Yes, Bhaiya."

Suraj sat down on a wooden log, opened the chamber of his gun, retrieved the blank cartridge and blew into the opening of the barrel to clean it. Chandar was still standing. Barre Sarkar looked up at him with his large eyes and Chandar bolted from there.

Barre Sarkar inserted a new cartridge and clicked the chamber shut. Chandni was so startled that she jumped as if a bullet had just struck her chest. Suraj leaned against the tree trunk. As the tree moved, Chandni stumbled and almost fell on her face, but steadied herself quickly. First she saw the barrel of the gun appear, then a hand and shoulder moved from behind the tree trunk. She tiptoed to the other side, but the barrel of the gun moved just as quickly and came back in a circle to face her. Chandni was shaking, sweat poured down her body. She turned swiftly with the intention of fleeing but became rooted to the ground, motionless as a statue. The barrel of the gun was pointed at her like a cobra's head.

Two deep wells, at the bottom of which were bullets. She tore her gaze away from the gun's barrel and looked fearfully into something even more dangerous—eyes, poisonous, like steel rods—and saw flames of hate and anger leaping at her. Despite her efforts she couldn't free herself from the vortex of his gaze.

She was stunned when the hissing snakes suddenly lowered their heads. Barre Sarkar's forehead was covered in sweat. The barrel of the gun was lowered. It seemed that a mountain had toppled over Barre Sarkar. His tall, thin body swayed, his shoulders drooped, his legs seemed to have turned into crunched-up paper, and he almost crumpled as he bowed before her.

If a hunter becomes helpless in the presence of the doe he has been stalking, then she too forgets her readiness to take flight. But in the next instant Chandni roused herself, jumped over the barrel of the gun and bolted towards the haveli.

4

"Nothing will ever come of it, Masiji. Give up hope of ever growing flowers on this rock."

Munshiji continued with his jibes. Masi was arranging Barre Sarkar's breakfast. When she called out to Usha the girl came running, dressed as she was. This behaviour will definitely help you become a queen! She was immediately made to turn around, go back and change. Munshiji laughed sarcastically and continued teasing Masi.

"Keep barking, you wretch—now even you think you can give yourself airs," Masi said angrily.

"But I'm saying all this for your own good. Why are you letting your daughter's youth wither away? Will you suspend her from the branch for the rest of her life? Parrots and birds will peck away at the fruit until it is hollow."

"Look here, Munshiji, don't meddle in my affairs."

"But I have to say there's something strange going on. I swear I have been standing guard here for seventeen years and nothing has happened yet."

"You wretch, what gibberish is this?"

"You're a woman, what can I say? But tell me the truth, have you ever heard that Barre Sarkar has teased the cleaning girl or pinched the washerwoman's bottom?"

"A curse on you, you wretch, do you think he's depraved like you? Will a Thakur's son flirt with the cleaning girl and the washerwoman?"

"Well, dear lady, don't say that. We all know about the nobility of the Thakurs. You remember the time of Barre Thakur? Not a single street was neglected."

"That's why he rotted away. My Suraj is not like that. You won't understand him, Munshi. Men with such devoutness and piety don't have any deceit in their hearts." Masi drew a long sigh.

"Well, all right, let's forget the cleaning girl and the washerwoman. Take our Usha Rani, beauty that would make the gods drool, but has Barre Sarkar ever flirted with her?"

"How dare you take my daughter's name? Bastard, get out of here!" Masi picked up her slipper and Munshiji ducked hastily.

"All right, all right, don't get so angry, but I still say something is wrong. What kind of piety and devotion is this, anyway? Does our Usha Rani say anything to any of her friends? Dear lady, this Vishwamitra looks like a wooden owl to me. Why are you praying to Sarna Devi all the time? She has no sway over this devotee."

The slipper hit his ankle with a whack and, screaming and cursing, he dashed out.

"Hey Ram, I'm dead," he howled in pain.

5

"Keep your wits about you, Munshiji."

All dressed up, Usha Rani was walking in from the other direction and thought Munshi was trying to tease her again.

Munshiji became enraged. "To hell with these slippers!" He kicked the slipper with force. "You will have to pay for my patience, mother and daughter, remember that!" And limping, muttering angrily, he left the room.

Dressed in pink, Usha Rani looked graceful and beautiful. Not twenty-seven years old at all. The glow of shyness and reticence on her face only enhanced her beauty.

Carrying a heavy breakfast tray she tiptoed into the room to find Barre Sarkar bent over his table, a hunting knife open in his hand. Before him lay a badly damaged picture of a naked woman. Usha screamed and the tray fell from her hands.

Startled, Barre Sarkar spun around to look at her. Usha saw that the person in front of her was not the god of her heart's temple, but Satan. His fang-like teeth sticking out, his eyes filled with a wild madness.

"Why are you here?" Barre Sarkar threw the knife down violently on the table and crushed the picture.

"Break…fast…" Usha stammered. Trembling and hiding her face in her hands, she turned to leave.

"Usha." He got up apprehensively. Usha stopped.

"Usha, come here," he said gently.

"Yes," Usha said, turning around.

"You…you…why do you take all this trouble?"

"But what's wrong? Whether I bring it or the servant, it's the same thing."

"I don't like it."

Usha did not respond and, wiping her tears, walked towards the door.

"Listen."

She stopped again.

"You're not upset about what I said, are you?" Barre Sarkar asked, looking at the waste-paper basket from the corner of his eyes.

"No, what is there to be upset about? It was my fault that the tray fell from my hands."

"Actually, I was very worried. This picture…"

"Yes?"

"Chandar's behaviour has left me very distressed. I don't know why his head is full of all this filth, where he gets these obscene pictures from."

Oh! He must have confiscated the picture from Chandar. Once when she was tidying up Barre Sarkar's desk she had seen some among his papers. She felt very angry with Chandar. The wretch! Barre Sarkar was right, such pictures should only be cut up and thrown away.

After Usha left Barre Sarkar collapsed on the table. The scratches made by the knife on its surface rose and quivered like hot flesh. His entire body was drenched in sweat.

Exhausted, he clenched his fists against his temples and broke into sobs.

6

Panting, gasping, Chandni fell on the bed and started crying. She felt as if her whole body had been bloodied. There was not a scratch on it but the feeling that she was taking her last breath stroked her heart with icy fingers.

What if someone had come, had seen?

If Chandar had seen them she would have died. That would be the end.

Luckily, just then the horse escaped from the stables and appeared on the lawn and all the servants ran after it. If that hadn't happened, the red flowers of her blood would have been blooming all over the pure white carpet in the lounge. She was running down the stairs, her foamy dupatta flying behind her. She had books in one hand and with the other she was trying to keep the dupatta in place, but as she gave it a tug it escaped from her grasp. When she turned around to pick it up, her hand flew up and the books fell from her other hand. On top of the stairs stood Barre Sarkar and her dupatta was fluttering in his hand.

Long snakes uncoiled from the sockets of his eyes and began to envelop her. There was a hunting knife in his hand, and with a slight twist of his wrist he was twirling her dupatta around it.

"Are you very frightened?" he asked, bending over her and touching the button on her shirt with the tip of his knife. Slowly he took her hand and placed the edge of the knife on it, but instead of going through her palm, the knife began to crawl over her wrist. Then, travelling up her arm, its tip rested at her throat.

The sharpness of ice shot all the way to Chandni's soul. She stood still, her eyes lowered, her breath held. The knife moved expertly and the top button of her shirt snapped and rolled down the stairs with a pinging sound.

One by one all the buttons were snipped off with a light movement. Huge tears kept falling soundlessly down her cheeks. The strength of her hands hanging by her side had been sapped. The icy tip of the knife halted exactly at the beating of her heart. A fiery drill tore through the depths of her soul. Silent explosions began going off in her head.

Before the volcano could erupt and she was reduced to ashes the horse escaped from the stables and began to create a commotion on the lawn. Suddenly it was as if the world had awakened. Drained, Chandni crouched on the stairs. She didn't see where Barre Sarkar had vanished, didn't know whether it was actually him or his ghost, whether all this had been manufactured by her troubled thoughts, a trick that had vanished in an instant.

Whom can she tell? And what will she say? How can an ant accuse an exalted god? Who is her witness and who her supporter? Pimo was her friend, she adored her, but would she be willing to tolerate this insult to Barre Bhaiya?

Barre Sarkar hates her because he is afraid that Chandar might develop a relationship with her and besmirch the name of the Thakurs. She is a lowly creature, the result of someone's sin no doubt, which is why she had been abandoned on a rubbish heap.

Once again she felt a bullet hit her chest. In front of her, in the big hall, Barre Sarkar's photo in the golden frame was sparkling. In front of the picture were flowers and the fragrance holder with cold embers.

Every day Usha Rani would pick fresh flowers and place them before the picture, take the offering with oil lamp, circle the room, then place it at its base.

Chandni wanted to pick up a large stone and hurl it at the picture. Her mouth became dry with anger and hatred, as if it was filled with ash all the way down to her throat.

Suddenly it seemed to her that the picture was smiling, that the poison-filled eyes were dancing. She turned around and ran, speeding down the stairs, and bumped into Chandar.

"What's the matter, ji?" Chandar steadied her.

"Hai, Chandarji." She placed her lips on his chest and burst into tears. Chandar immediately took advantage of the situation. There was such pleasure, such sweetness in his love—Chandni melted.

"Hey Ram, Chandru, devour me, let me drown in you." The intensity of her love made her tremble. Sparks flew in her head when she was close to Chandar, but that was also when she felt really angry with him. She had no control over the desire to simultaneously sink into him and run away from him. The fifteen year-old Chandni became terrified when she couldn't find the answers to many of life's questions. An unknown fear impelled her to flee from the joy of Chandar's love, but when she was apart from him her heart was filled with longing.

Very soon Chandar made her laugh. The frightened Chandni of a few minutes earlier was quickly transformed into a coquettish beauty. Sprinting like a doe, laughing freely and taking shortcuts through the lawn, she clambered up the veranda to the dining room. It was dark inside, a dim light streaming through the windows. Chandar stumbled over a flower-pot and fell, but ran laughing towards the gallery. She spun around to look and knew from the sound of Chandar's footsteps that there was no escaping him, he would certainly catch her. The moment she turned to move towards the staircase two powerful hands manacled her. She felt a burning cobra mouth on her lips and the poison, hissing and spitting, seeped into her being…down… down…She felt as if she had reached the absolute bottom, would never get her breath back. In the distance the sound of Chandar's footsteps was slowly fading away. Chandar…Chandar the moon… with every ounce of her being she pulled herself up from the abyss, dashed towards Chandar and fell on her face in front of him.

"Arre, what happened?" he said, alarmed by her terror-stricken expression.

"There…he…" Her eyes were wide open and her voice suffocated.

"What is it, you silly girl?" Chandar went in and looked around the gallery. Leaning against the column was Barre Sarkar. The devilish look on his face startled Chandar as well.

"Arre, Barre Bhaiya, she's crazy, this Chandni, took fright when she saw you!" Chandar laughed sheepishly and pushed Chandni away from him. Then he began scratching his head like a fool. He had a cigarette in his other hand which he quickly thrust into his pocket.

Chandni tried to say something, but seeing the look on Chandar's face she turned and ran, sobbing. When Chandar tried to slip away as well, Barre Sarkar said in a very sombre voice, "Chandar."

"Yes." Chandar flinched.

"I have to talk to you. Please come with me."

Chandar trembled at the severity of his tone but said nothing and followed him obediently.

"Sit down." Barre Sarkar gestured and then started pacing back and forth restlessly. Chandar was sweating, he wanted to sneak out and not show his face again for many days, and surely afterwards Barre Sarkar would have forgotten everything.

Suddenly Barre Bhaiya stopped pacing and stared intently at Chandar, as if he would devour him whole.

"Here." He offered Chandar his cigarette case in a surprise gesture.

"Ji…oh no…" Chandar stammered.

"Well, as you please. Perhaps it's more fun to smoke surreptitiously." When Barre Bhaiya was angry he would adopt a more formal mode of address.

"Do you love Chandni?"

"Ji…ji…no…ji…." Chandar cringed. He was unprepared for such a frontal attack.

"Don't make a fool of me by lying!" Barre Bhaiya roared. "Your behaviour is becoming increasingly intolerable." This was something else he did when he was angry, he resorted to speaking in English.

Chandar's head dropped further with each word. Barre Bhaiya was delivering his lecture without pausing. The idea that he was in love with Chandni was not new to Chandar, Pimo teased him constantly about it. Masi had also taunted him, and as for Usha Rani, she had nearly sealed the matter. But he always made light of it and avoided speaking about it seriously.

He had not yet felt the need to marry. But hearing Barre Bhaiya bring up the subject so abruptly unnerved him.

"What have I done wrong, Chandar?"

"Ji?" Chandar was so distracted he hadn't heard what Barre Bhaiya said.

"Have I ever done anything that would bring harm to you, to Parmila or any other member of this household?"

"No, Barre Bhaiya."

"Have I not fulfilled my duty faithfully? Have I done you an injustice of some sort? When have I given you reason to complain?"

"No, you've never been unjust, Barre Bhaiya."

"Then what crime are you punishing me for?"

"Me? I, Barre Bhaiya…" Chandar whimpered and started thinking of ways to make his escape.

"Do you know how this despicable action of yours will affect the family? What will the world say? You…love her, don't lie. She has taken control of your brain and your heart like an evil spirit, you've lost your senses, and you're quivering like a fish caught in a net. A lowly ant has compelled a mountain to lower itself at her feet. Do you know the family you belong to? You are Surya Vanshi and she…she's an unidentified, base creature about whose parentage nothing is known, who in all likelihood is the fruit of some ignominious person's act. Do you want to stain the family name by marrying her, are you blind, don't you know how all this will end? You will become mad…mad…ma."

Suddenly Barre Sarkar jumped back…he was foaming at the mouth and standing in front of the mirror, chastising himself. Filled with dread, he turned to look at Chandar and saw that the chair was empty. Who knows when Chandar had slipped out of the room.

"Oh, Bhagwan! Bhagwan!" He held his head in his hands and slumped to the floor. "What have I done to deserve such an awful punishment?" Who knows how long he smouldered alone in the conflagration his mind had created, how long he suffered its turmoil.

7

A wave of hot blood surged in Barre Sarkar's head, the pen shook in his hands and the red embers in his eyes began to dance.

"You...you like her?" he asked Munshiji in a choked voice.

"Ji...ji, Sarkar. The girl is a firecracker, strikes you on the heart with a loud thud. And then I have eaten your salt, and even if you make shoes with my skin and wear them I will consider myself fortunate. Chote Sarkar is getting out of hand." He placed more papers in front of Suraj for his signature. "You will not have to worry and I..." Munshiji spoke as if a rasgulla was dissolving in his mouth.

"And you..." The veins in Barre Sarkar's neck became taut like steel, his temples throbbed and his nostrils flared.

"Ji, Sarkar, how long can I carry on alone! In three or four years she'll be strong like a she-goat and then there'll be trouble. Masiji is already losing sleep over her. If Chote Sarkar makes some kind of a slip there will be no help for it. And it's not his fault. The girl is full of wiles, she can make the best of them sweat, Sarkar, and Chote Sarkar is so naive. That's why I thought, when else will I be of use? Ram knows whether she's the offspring of a bhangi or a chamar, but Sir, I am your very loyal servant so what does it matter if..."

"You want to...marry her?"

"Ji...the matter will end here, no one will have the audacity to say or suggest anything."

"You are...you like her?" Barre Sarkar ground his teeth, demons began dancing in his eyes, his mouth tightened. Suddenly Munshiji's laugh froze on his lips. He drew back with a start, but like an angry lion Barre Sarkar leapt up and grabbed his neck.

"Sir, I made a mistake, Sarkar!" Munshiji freed himself from his grip and, falling on his feet, he began begging forgiveness right there. Suddenly Barre Sarkar retreated in shock.

"I understand, I understand, Sarkar…How would I know…" Munshiji got up and, fixing his dhoti hastily, put his hands together.

"Know what?" Barre Sarkar turned around and hissed. "Nothing, Sir, nothing at all."

"What do you understand, you wretch?"

"Nothing. Sarkar, I understand nothing. What can I know? I… I…" Flabbergasted, Munshiji ran from the room and bumped into Usha Rani on his way out.

"Arre, a curse on you!" he swore at the long folds of his dhoti which were getting entangled between his legs. "Ram, Ram, hey Shri Ram, what unkindness!"

Usha had witnessed only the scolding, and that made her happy. She laughed and said, "Arre, Munshiji, have you lost your mind, do you want to die? Why else would you try to get familiar with him?"

"To hell with getting familiar! Ram Ram, this is too much. What a—Bhagwan…one can't even trust sadhus and saints anymore, I swear."

"Arre, what happened?" Masi asked, "Barre Sarkar has never lifted a finger against anyone. This dog must have said something really terrible to make him lose his temper."

"What could it be, a curse on you!" Munshiji muttered angrily.

"All right, that's enough. You had better pack your things and get ready to leave."

"Arre, death to those who will pack and leave! I say, think about yourself now. Forget all your dreams of becoming the mother queen. What queen, consider yourself lucky if you find a place in this house that will provide you a roof over your head."

"What is all this nonsense, are you mad?"

"This is not nonsense, my queen, listen to me and think about your well-being. Arre, he's the lord and master and can do what he wants and no one can question him, but I have to say the girl is a poisonous thorn."

"Which girl?"

"Arre, please don't ask me, if you have eyes, see for yourself. Hey Bhagwan, the signs are not good, everything will be turned upside down, a violent Mahabharat will take place, brother will devour brother."

"Oh, you are so disagreeable," Usha Rani said angrily and went inside.

Drenched in sweat, Barre Sarkar sat with his head down on the desk. His whole body was wracked with sobs. Usha Rani was badly shaken, seeing such a dignified man shattered like a broken toy. The maternal instinct that had lain dormant in her was aroused, she felt like taking his sorrow-laden head to her breast, but shyness and reticence stood in her way.

Barre Sarkar lifted his head. There was an ocean of pain raging in his eyes. His lips began to quiver like a defeated, whimpering child. He looked at Usha like a beggar scorned, then became agitated. He wanted to fling himself at her feet and say: "Usha Rani, save me. Save me from the cobras in this terrifying cave. Place your pure lips once on my throbbing forehead and all my sins will be washed away." But Barre Sarkar had learned to conceal his pain. At the place where he had arrived there was no companion, no friend, just him and his isolation. Immediately he became conscious of his status. Flexed his neck and spoke arrogantly, "What is it?"

"What are your wishes regarding Munshiji?"

"Munshiji? Give Munshiji two hundred rupees for some winter clothes."

"But…" Usha Rani was speechless.

"Tell Gopal to bring me my tea on the terrace," he said curtly.

"This…the…Munshiji…"

"What do you want to say about Munshiji?"

"I mean that…"

"Are you upset at the way I treated him?" he asked brusquely. "If that is the case, I'm sorry. I thought you didn't like him."

"Yes."

"But it appears that I was wrong." Barre Sarkar started acting.

"I…I don't understand."

"He wants to marry you. If you're willing, then…"

"No!" Usha Rani exclaimed, holding back her tears.

"But if you want to, then…" He enjoyed upsetting her, he felt this gave him some relief from his own misery.

"No, of course not!" Usha Rani burst into tears.

"Oh. Well, that's what I thought and that's why I scolded him, but I got angrier than I should have."

"You did the right thing," Usha Rani said passionately.

"No, I didn't do the correct thing at all. I have no right to place obstacles in the path of your marriage." Barre Sarkar continued to mislead Usha Rani and she quivered like a fish that has swallowed the bait. As if she was a football and Barre Sarkar was playing with her emotions.

"Give him the money in cash and take these papers as well. Tell him he can do what he thinks is appropriate. I'm not feeling well, I lose my temper easily at the slightest thing." When he had had his fill he changed the topic with careless indifference.

Hey Bhagwan! My lord is so great. Hai, is there anyone who feels so sorry for having beaten a servant, especially a pig like Munshiji, who doesn't know when to hold his tongue.

In the meantime, while Usha Rani went to find out what Barre Sarkar had in mind for Munshiji, Munshiji had not retreated. He stood with his ear to the door, but hearing Barre Sarkar's instructions, swore roundly and became giddy with joy. When Usha Rani appeared at the door he put on a serious face and asked, "Raniji, what's my punishment?"

Usha threw a furious look at him and, incensed, walked away.

Munshiji constantly mourned Usha's wasted youth. He was unmarried and knew well the taste of solitude. He was Barre Sarkar's age, had no family of his own, and had never taken any interest in getting married. His salary, every single penny of it, had been saved. He had been admiring Usha from a distance for a long time, but after hearing Barre Sarkar's remarks, felt his courage return.

As was her custom, Masi completed Barre Sarkar's aarti and then, holding the tray in her hand, sat down on the floor near him.

"My son, Usha Rani is getting older, it's time you did something about her marriage."

"Of course, of course. We shouldn't delay any longer. You can do whatever is best. What is the young man like? Don't worry about money, the groom should be suitable."

"But...but my son...your mother wanted her to stay in this house," Masi stammered.

"When did I say she shouldn't live here? All the rooms in the west wing are vacant, bring a son-in-law who will be willing to stay with his in-laws. What does the young man do?"

Masiji couldn't restrain herself and burst into tears.

"My son, you are everything for Usha, I have pinned all my hopes on you."

"Oh, Masi, I'm so sorry, I have been remiss, and you know how useless I am, I don't meet anyone, don't go anywhere. It's not easy finding a husband for Usha Rani. The man should be decent, worthy. By the way, Masi, what do you think about Munshiji?"

Barre Bhaiya skirted the issue with such skill that Masi was left in a state of complete shock.

"Munshi? That worthless upstart! Is he the only one left for my daughter? I would rather fling her into a well! Whoever marries my beautiful, gracious girl will be blessed with good fortune. My son, the special attachment Usha has for this family is no secret. How she has adorned and organised this house. It is her house, that's why."

"I know, Masi. All right, don't worry. By the grace of Bhagwan, all will be well. Let me take care of the harvest first. This year we haven't had enough rain. Arre, Munshiji..."

He tried to dodge the issue again.

Munshiji, who had been eavesdropping, appeared immediately. "Ji, Sarkar," he said smiling coyly like a bride.

"Just check that new tractor, it's not working properly. Aali is so incompetent, he doesn't understand anything, he's also very lazy."

"No, Sarkar, he's not lazy, he's scared. He says if the bosom of the earth bears so much weight, how will anything grow on it."

"What nonsense! And the oxen and the plough have no weight? The fool. Munshiji."

"Ji, Sarkar."

"Can you recommend a boy?"

"Ji, Sarkar, for cleaning and dusting the house?" Munshiji was befuddled.

"No, no, not for cleaning and dusting; to marry, for Usha Rani."

Masiji didn't wait to hear the rest and stormed out of the room. Barre Sarkar felt exhilarated. He heaved a sigh of relief and broke into a smile, but the moment he noticed Munshiji smiling too, he assumed a stern look. "Yes?"

"Ji…ji, Sarkar!" Munshiji said, bemused.

"What is it?"

"Ji, Sarkar, you called me."

"Oh, I did call you, but that doesn't mean that once you're here you have to remain here like a ton of bricks on my head!"

Munshiji retreated hastily like a dog that has received a beating from its master. Barre Sarkar regarded his behaviour as a mark of his superiority over others. He had developed a dislike for Masi. He wasn't really interested in Chandni, he had just begun to feel that life without a woman was barren and so had thought, if not Usha Rani, then Chandni would do. She was an Untouchable no doubt, one doesn't find the children of goddesses lying on heaps of garbage, but at least she was a woman. Today's events put a seal on Munshiji's suspicions.

Hai Ram, who knows what is about to happen in this haveli? Will the sun and moon clash? There will be a terrible explosion. This girl must be a niece of Menaka, which is why she has come to destroy Barre Sarkar, a man of Vishwamitra's stature. Here he is, a god, and she a sinful woman.

"Just stop, your god be cursed," he muttered, and looking around, swore heavily at many others as well.

Masiji, Barre Sarkar, and life's drab solitude.

8

"No, no, Pimo Rani, I feel shy."

"Now stop, you silly girl, what's there to be shy about?" Pimo said, patting her lovingly on the head.

"But no one knows the correct date of my birth."

"Look, the day we found you is the day of your birth. You probably don't remember, Usha Devi made such shining new clothes for you. There hasn't been a year since then that we haven't celebrated your birthday, so why make such a fuss now?"

"It just doesn't seem nice. I've been treated so well, isn't that enough?"

"Chandni, you're very mean, you're always talking about being brought up here. I've been raised in this house as well, Chandar and I don't always keep complaining about that."

"But you're the children of this family!"

"And Usha Didi?"

"She has been doing the work of ten people since she was a young girl. I'm useless."

"If she works, it's not as a favour to anyone. After she gets married to our brother she will become the mistress of the house."

"By Ram's grace, may she get married to Barre Sarkar soon." Chandni began praying fervently. "I bend my forehead before Gori Mayya every day and pray for this to happen."

"And you don't pray for your own wedding? You wait, I'll tell Chot Bhaiya that Chandni doesn't love you one bit!"

"Arre, what? Of course I do!"

"Ram, Ram, what a shameless girl, telling me openly that you're crazy about my brother."

"Stop it now, why would I be crazy about him?"

"But he's crazy about you…"

"Look, Pimo, stop teasing me. What about you—all day long you're writing letters to Prakash ji."

"Unh! How can one trust a man who is thousands of miles away? What if he finds someone to fall in love with there?" Pimo had got engaged to a doctor who was now in England. "Leave my story alone, did you remind Chot Bhaiya about the necklace?"

"Arre, the poor fellow can't afford it, Ram only knows how expensive it is."

"So what? It will always be in his wife's possession."

"Don't tease me, please, you'll make me cry."

"Why? Where will the moon's moonlight go and—"

"She'll die, the wretch!" Chandni collapsed face down on the bed.

But Chandar was running around in a state of consternation. Fulfilling the demand for a two hundred and fifty rupee necklace was no joke. But he had a share in the family's wealth as well, surely Bhaiya wouldn't refuse? He felt awkward asking it for Chandni. He asked Usha Didi, but she could spare only a hundred. He had about fifty or sixty. A hundred and fifty was not enough.

Finally he was forced to approach Bhaiya.

"Bhaiya, can I have some money?" he said, standing behind him.

"Money?"

"Some rupees."

"How many rupees?"

"About two hundred or two hundred and fifty."

"Why do you suddenly need money?"

"I…I ordered a tennis racket and I have to pay the freight… and…"

Barre Sarkar seethed at Chandar's lie. He had eavesdropped on the conversation in the house about the necklace. Pimo said if Chandar didn't buy the necklace Chandni would not talk to him for the rest of her life. Well, forget the rest of their lives, if this laughter and hilarity, this kissing and hugging in corners was interrupted for even a few days it wouldn't be such a bad thing.

"I have about ten or twelve rupees with me and the bank is closed now," he replied curtly.

Chandar wiped the sweat from his forehead and departed.

After Chandar had left, Suraj got up calmly. The safe was stuffed with bundles of rupees that had come in for land taxes. Picking up a fat wad he slipped it into his pocket and came out looking very dignified, asked the driver to bring the car around and getting in, drove off.

Chandar sat down on the stairs with his head between his hands. What should he do? Pimo won't give him a penny. And if Chandni found out that he was collecting money from here and there for the necklace, she wouldn't speak to him. Actually, she herself had been telling him not to get it, it was Pimo who insisted, saying Chandni didn't have any real jewellery. She or Usha Devi would force her to wear something of theirs on festivals. Pimo taunted him so much that he was determined to demonstrate his gallantry. It would be a real disaster if the necklace failed to materialise now.

Pimo was all dressed up and ready for her dance practice. Chandar grabbed her on the stairs.

"Arre, Pimoji, I saw someone do something extraordinary today."

"Who?"

"A magician."

"Magician?"

"Yes, he came to our college. I learned a trick from him."

"Oh?" Pimo started walking.

"Do you want to see some magic?"

"No, no."

"Why not, you silly girl?" Chandar got annoyed.

"Arre, my tonga is waiting, I'll be late."

"All we need is two minutes." He pulled Pimo to the stairs and made her sit down.

"Now, take out a note."

"No."

"Arre, come on, I'll turn it into two."

Pimo finally took out a one-rupee note.

"*Come on Kalkatte-wali, may your attack not fail, ant-sant, bijli basant*...here blow." Pimo blew gingerly, Chandar opened his fist. Instead of one rupee there was a ten-rupee note in his hand.

Pimo screamed. "Oh my, Chandar Bhaiya!"

"Come one, let's quickly change all of them."

"No, no, that's enough." Pimo calmly put the money into her purse and got up.

"Arre, arre, where are you running off to?" Chandar pulled her down again. "You'll regret it later, I swear, come on, take out the money." Chandar clicked his fingers.

Pimo took out the ten-rupee note.

"Why are you dawdling like this? I can't sit here forever and keep blowing the magic words one by one on ten-rupee notes. Give me a hundred rupee note and I'll change it to a thousand."

"Really?"

"Oh, yes."

"A thousand?"

"Of course. And if it's a thousand, I'll change it to ten thousand."

"I don't have a thousand rupee note."

"All right, let's have the hundred." Chandar got hold of the money and began blowing on it quickly. *"Kali Kalkatte-wali, chal chaal,* come on blow, do it properly, what's this *phoo, phoo,* remember if you don't blow properly the whole thing can be reversed."

Pimo blew on his fist with all her might. When Chandar opened it she saw a fragment of paper on his palm.

"You see?"

"Hai Ram! My hundred-rupee note."

"What can I do now? I was telling you, silly girl, blow properly, blow properly please, but." Chandar roared.

"I don't care, I want my money back!"

"Ahaha, you didn't blow the right way and the magic worked backwards, so what can I do? I'm getting late, out of my way." He pushed her aside and tried to leave.

"Oh no, how will I pay the dance master? Give me back my hundred rupees. Here are your ten rupees."

"Arre, I performed my magic right in front of you and now you're complaining. My dear, this is magic, sometimes it works and sometimes it fails." Chandar assumed an innocent expression and took the ten-rupee note as well. "Don't worry, I'm going out for just a while. When I come back I'll change all your money and make it grow ten times over."

"You wretch, I'm not going to be deceived by your tricks again." Pimo understood Chandar's tricks very well, but if he had asked openly for the money she would never have given him a penny.

9

The haveli was lit up with electric lights. Everyone knew that Chandni's birthday was just an excuse. The inhabitants of this haveli would even celebrate the birthday of a dog. Life's monotony and weariness are banished for a short while, there's a bit of excitement, Usha Devi gets a chance to show off her cooking skills, an effective way of impressing Barre Sarkar.

Chandni was pacing restlessly in her room, waiting anxiously for Chandar. When she saw his bicycle coming around the bend towards the gate, she dashed out.

"Chandarji, my necklace!" She was startled to see his sad, forlorn face. "What happened?" She shrank back.

"The necklace was sold."

"It was sold?"

"Yes. Someone came and bought it half an hour ago, but the jeweller has promised he'll make the same necklace in about fifteen days."

"Fifteen days!" She became tearful and turned to go.

"Listen, Channo..."

"I don't want to listen," she yelled. "I've been telling you it's going to be sold, but you wouldn't listen."

"A second one will be made...then..."

"I don't want a second, third, fourth or fifth. If you get it, I swear I'll smash it with a stone!"

"Chandra Rani..."

"Don't you dare call me Chandra Rani! I'm not a rani, I'm an orphaned girl left on a pile of garbage. If I had been a rani you wouldn't have dared to not get the necklace for me. The person for whom somebody else has bought the necklace is the real rani." Her face was streaked with tears.

Barre Sarkar stood observing this poignant drama and was overjoyed. No one noticed his smirking. He had been turning the necklace around in his hand for the last two hours.

Every year he used to hand out money on birthdays through Munshiji. How was he going to give Chandni the necklace? He paced for hours trying to figure out a way to do it. What would he say? How would he say it? Should he give it to her in front of everyone or in private? All he wanted was to see her smile light up her face when she saw the necklace.

Chandar, who thought of him as a father, whom he loved more than his life—how much he loved him! And how much he hated him! In his waking and sleeping hours he dreamt about his death. Chandar falls from the horse, his brains are crushed, he has lifted up the broken, sorrowing Chandni to his parched lips and— and he would wake up! His throat dry, bathed in sweat, he would shiver in exhaustion. How many times had he killed Chandar in his imagination? Trampling over his blood-soaked body he had entered the bridal chamber and, and then he would awaken, his heart would sink, he would sob bitterly. Chandar…his little brother!

"My dear son, you are now father to both Chandar and Pimo, don't ever cause them pain, otherwise my soul will roam forever restlessly," his mother had said on her deathbed, and from that day on he had sacrificed his childhood and donned the prickly garment of maturity and responsibility. But nature was determined to ruin his plan, an unknown power was making him dance like a puppet, his entire life's piousness and goodness were being annihilated in one stroke.

At night he was woken abruptly by frightening nightmares. Turning the lights on he would search frantically for blood stains on his clothes. When that didn't reassure him he would go to Chandar's room and look at his sleeping form, trying to ensure he didn't have any wounds, that he was breathing normally. Seeing him alive and well he would fix his blanket, tuck his mosquito net in properly. If Chandar woke up suddenly he would joke, "Oh Bhaiya, I'm not a child!"

"There's malaria spreading in the wetlands. You're very careless."

When the two brothers sat next to each other, they spoke affectionately, reminisced about the loving care of their parents. This was when Chandni was far from their thoughts and Barre Sarkar would make plans for Chandar's grand future, estimate Pimo's wedding expenses, generously dole out money to Chandar, as if he were applying a balm to wounds that he had inflicted on him, although these wounds cut just as deeply into his own heart.

But right now, he was anxious to witness the interesting drama of Chandar's defeat and his own victory. When he came down with the necklace the scene before him was quite unexpected. The same Chandni who had been so enraged a while ago was melting in Chandar's arms.

"My Chand Raja, your arms are my real necklace. A curse on the necklace! How stupid can I be? Wah, Chandar Raja will one day put a diamond-studded necklace around my neck. Yes, Chandar?"

"But to this day I've never given you anything." Chandar sat with his head lowered in shame.

"You gave me my life, you silly boy. You gave me what Bhagwan had snatched from me—this house, happiness, a friend like Pimo... what else do I need? And when you look at me like this, my being is clothed with pearls. Don't look at me, Chandar." She placed her hand over his eyes.

A fire flared in Barre Sarkar's being, he began to breathe heavily like a wild boar, poisonous arrows swam through his eyes and pierced his temples, the necklace stung his fingers like a snake. But before he could attack his rival like a wild animal, someone's footsteps behind him stopped him.

Usha Rani was coming down the stairs slowly, all dressed up.

"Usha." He swallowed the bitterness in his throat and called out to her in the sweetest of tones.

Ahh! Hearing her name on his lips, Usha felt as if a bullet had struck her bosom. Pulling herself together she said, "Ji."

"Please come here," he said, greatly enjoying her discomfort.

Usha felt life slipping from her. Like a new bride, she walked towards him. Hey Bhagwan, he had uttered her name today!

"Look what I've got for you."

"For me?"

"Yes, a small little gift." He dangled the necklace in front of her.

"The most beautiful adornment of my life," she said softly and spread out her hands.

"Unhun. I'll put it on myself."

"Oh, so you bought this necklace?" Chandar spoke up before Chandni could stop him.

"Yes. Why? Don't you like it?"

"No, no, I mean, yes," Chandar said tonelessly.

Suddenly Masi arrived on the scene and burst into tears. "Live long, my beloved son, live long always, may you have my life too," making the gesture for removing the evil eye. Then she embraced Usha and began crying loudly, as though the bride's palanquin was ready and she was about to depart for her in-laws'.

A storm of anger and hate raged in Barre Sarkar, but he controlled himself.

"Oh yes, Ushaji, please tell Munshiji to give Chandni money for her birthday, whatever she got last time," he said coldly and walked towards the library.

"I don't want any money," Chandni hissed. For a while their spirits fell, but they soon forgot everything and got busy with the birthday revelry. Boys and girls were making a racket on the lawn, the place echoed with the tinkle of laughter. A new kind of glow shone in Usha Rani's eyes today. Again and again she gently caressed the necklace and then blushed.

Masi was in a strange frame of mind. On the one hand she was burning with jealousy because of the attention Chandni was getting, but at the same time she was happy that Chandar was completely overpowered by her. The moment he marries her Barre Sarkar will cut him off from the family's assets. He is the master, everything is in his name.

Barre Sarkar was alone in all this commotion. Rancour and malice rained on his thoughts, disappointment and misery stifled him, the desolation in his heart grew. Like an idiot he pinned his gaze on Chandar and Chandni. Every joyful gesture of theirs lashed his emotions like a whip.

Suddenly he noticed the necklace glinting in the grass. It had probably slipped from Usha's neck after its clasp came undone. He bent and picked it up and was about to give it to Usha when he paused, as if held back by something. Then he got up. Chandni's purse was lying on the table. He opened it quietly and slipped the necklace inside.

10

Chandni lay motionless on a pile of dead leaves under the molsri tree. She would come and sit here whenever she felt her heart was breaking. This is where Chandar had found her. This is where she would lie until she dried up like the leaves and the gardener would sweep her up with his jharu made of brambles and burn her with the rest of the garbage. Her ashes would permeate the air and fly from one lifetime to another.

In the past whenever Chandni was upset, Chandar would quickly appease her. But this time when he saw her lying on the leaves, he ignored her. He had never been so angry.

When Usha Devi's necklace came out of Chandni's bag in the presence of all the guests, Chandar felt like sinking into the earth with shame. He slapped Chandni so hard in front of everyone that her face was still swollen. He wouldn't let her say one word in her defence.

"She must be the child of a thief or a bandit," Masi said, apologising for carrying out a search among the guests.

"Let it be, Masi," Barre Sarkar tried to intervene, but she wasn't one to stop.

Barre Sarkar said, "Uff-oh! Please let it go. It's human to make a mistake. Usha Rani shouldn't wear this necklace now."

"Why not?" Usha Rani trembled in trepidation.

"Give it to the person who likes it. I'll buy you another one."

"Why should she give it? Who does the girl think she is to want the necklace? I'll forfeit her any day. She's been raised on our leftovers and she tries to deceive us!"

"Masiji, I'll swear by anything you want me to, I did not touch the necklace." Overcome by shame, Chandni began to weep.

"Stop it, you wretch, who do you have in the world, dead or alive, by whom you can swear? If you had anyone, would you have been thrown on a rubbish heap? My daughter treated this bitch like her own sister, made all the arrangements for her birthday celebrations, dressed her up, and this is how she is repaid?"

"Chandni!" Pimo was sobbing. "You loved this necklace so much that you weren't afraid of stealing it? Chot Bhaiya!" She ran into Chandar's arms.

His eyes moist with tears, Chandar glanced at Chandni. She felt completely crushed. "Chandar, don't you trust me?"

And that was when Chandar slapped her hard and thrust her from him.

"Look, you are all making too much of this. She liked the necklace, she took it, what's so terrible about that? Chandar, you're being unfair." Barre Sarkar added fuel to the fire and as a result Chandni received further scoldings.

"You know, if someone likes the necklace so much that she has to steal it, then I don't want that necklace to be given to Usha. Usha, let Chandni have it."

"Oh, if I have to lose my life I will not give this necklace to anyone!" Usha said, choking, as if someone was stealing not just the necklace but her marital bliss.

"Yes, why should she give it away?" Masiji shouted. "If this wretch asks for someone's life should the great lady's wish be granted?"

The party broke up, the guests made hasty exits. It was as if someone had died. Chandar's tender heart had never suffered such a blow before. As for Chandni, she felt she no longer had reason to live. When the moon is covered by dark clouds, why will the moonlight not be extinguished?

Pimo argued, "If Chandni is a thief why doesn't she steal the jewellery that is always lying on my dressing table?"

"She stole to cover me with shame," Chandar said, swallowing hard.

"She's always coveting other people's things, she wanted to hurt me, she can't bear to see anyone happy," Usha whimpered.

"No, you don't know this miserable wretch!" Masi spewed out more poison. "She's actually jealous of Barre Sarkar. If she had her way she would have all the family wealth transferred to Chandar's name. He's crazy about her, isn't he?"

The only one who didn't scold Chandni was Barre Sarkar. He was a noble man, after all! How much compassion there was in his heart! He kept saying, "Such a terrible punishment for such a small transgression. This is unfair on Chandar's part."

He was a god. To forgive was a sign of greatness. Those whom Chandni regarded as her own turned out to be so cowardly, and he whom she regarded as her mortal enemy was trying to save her. Overnight her heart was washed clean of all the bad feelings she had nursed against him. If she hadn't been so scared of him she would have fallen at his feet this very instant.

My Sarkar, I misunderstood you, I'm a sinner, please forgive me, punish me as you see fit, but tell Chandar not to destroy me like this. I won't even be able to die without his love.

Ah, in this house where everyone had treated her so lovingly, there was no one now who wanted to look at her. Several times Pimo tried to approach her, but Masi made such a fuss that she didn't have the nerve to do it.

"You will be ruined in the company of this thief, this low caste girl," Masi shouted, and then threatened to move her bed to Usha's room. But Pimo felt stifled in Usha's room, and she couldn't stay away from Chandni either.

"Chandni, you wretch, why did you steal the necklace? I want to beat you to pulp." She couldn't restrain herself.

How much love there was in this reprimand! Chandni burst into tears. "Pimo Rani, I swear on your life, if I have touched the necklace I should be stricken with leprosy, I should die, I should be blinded."

"No, no, please don't talk like that. But this Chandar, he's such a killjoy. We had plans to go for a picnic on Sunday and that's all ruined now. One would think it's not a necklace, it's some spectre—the house looks desolate. I feel so depressed." So saying she went to Usha's room.

"Yes?"

"Please forgive me, Rani Didi."

"Forgive you for what?"

"That necklace of yours? I…I took it," Pimo said, rubbing her eyes.

"You took it?"

"Yes…and then…"

"And then?"

"I slipped it into the purse."

"Chandni's purse?"

"Of course. My purse was in my room."

"You're lying."

"Arre, it's the truth, my dearest Didi."

"Don't talk nonsense. Why would you steal it?"

"I did it for fun, I didn't steal it."

"Then why were you lying about it?"

"I picked it up, it was lying on the grass. I picked it up and put it in the bag. You weren't there."

"Hai Ram! Why didn't you tell me?"

"I…I was afraid that everyone would think I was a thief. Masi was so angry…I had gone to the bathroom and when I returned I saw that…Chandni had been accused of stealing," Pimo started stuttering.

"You're lying, didn't you also scold Chandni?"

"Well, what else could I do? Usha Didi, I was confused, I didn't know what to say."

"Hai Ram, this is terrible. All right, you witch, you stole the necklace and Chandni got the scolding for it. Why didn't you say something?"

"Well, Chandni had been quarrelling with me since that morning."

Chandar was livid when he was told. "And so you trapped her? Come on, you witch, let's go to Barre Bhaiya." He pulled her by her plait. "You'll see how I make him give you a thorough beating," pushing and pummelling her. Pimo kicked and struggled and then sat down, refusing to budge. Chandar lifted her up in his arms and dumped her like a gunny bag in front of Barre Bhaiya.

"Bhaiya, look what this witch has done!"

"Chandar, are you in your senses?"

"How can I remain in my senses? She's the one who stole the necklace and poor Chandni got the blame for it!"

"Parmila, what is all this?"

"Barre Bhaiya...I..."

"Stole the necklace and..."

"Chot Bhaiya, don't interrupt me. Barre Bhaiya, I put the necklace in Chandni's bag."

"You're a liar!" Barre Bhaiya shouted.

Pimo started weeping.

"But, Barre Bhaiya, she has admitted this herself."

"She's lying." Barre Bhaiya's eyes blazed in anger.

"No, Barre Bhaiya, she's saying she did it. Just think, is there anyone else who can be so stupid?"

"Yes...but..." Barre Bhaiya lowered his eyes.

"Please forgive me, Bhaiya. I hid the necklace as a joke. But when the situation became serious I got scared and kept my mouth shut."

"Pimo!"

"Ji, Barre Bhaiya."

"Come here."

"Ji, Barre Bhaiya."

"You know that lying is a sin."

"But Bhaiya, I can swear that Chandni didn't steal the necklace."

"Then who stole it?"

"I did." She lied, but there was not the slightest hint of hesitation in her clear and innocent gaze.

"No."

"Then who did it?"

"I did," Barre Sarkar said.

"You? Oh..." She burst out laughing. "Go on, Barre Bhaiya, you..." She couldn't control her laughter.

Chandar went and told Chandni that Pimo had admitted her crime, that she was the one who had placed the necklace in her purse.

"Pimo?" Chandni was startled.

"Yes. Probably because she was jealous that your birthday was being celebrated with such pomp."

"Ram, Ram, what are you saying, Chandarji! Pimo jealous of my happiness? She *is* my happiness. Bhagwan took away everything from me, gave me Pimo and I got everything back. This is the greatest wealth of my life."

"Arre, you don't know her, she's a real witch."

"No, no, she's lying."

"Arre, wah! What will she get by lying? A scolding?"

"Because…you don't know her, Chandarji…because she is as innocent and soft-hearted as a child, she's taken on all the blame."

"Then that means…you mean she didn't steal it and you did?"

"No, I didn't steal the necklace, but what difference does it make? You had already decided I was the culprit and punished me accordingly. What's the use of investigating now?"

"Chandni…"

But Chandni turned and walked away.

"Listen, Chandni." Chandar caught hold of her arm, but she shook him off.

"You won't talk to me for the rest of your life?"

"No." Chandni bit her lips.

"All right, we're not speaking to each other ever again?"

"Never."

"So you won't marry me?"

"Only if I wanted to die, would I marry someone mean like you who would never give me any respect!" Chandni made a face.

"So who will you marry?"

"Whomever I want."

"To hell with what you want! I'll shoot the bastard."

"Oh, who do you think you are to shoot anyone?"

"Watch what you say, Chandni—whom are you calling stupid?" Chandar shouted, advancing towards her.

"Yes, stupid!" Chandni turned and jumped over the drain.

"The worst kind of stupid person?" Chandar tripped her.

Chandni fell into the sludge flowing in the gutter. Gritting her teeth she picked up a handful and lobbed it at Chandar. Within a few minutes the two of them were grappling with each other in the muddy slush.

"What is going on?" Barre Sarkar asked. He was standing on the steps.

"Union!" Usha Rani broke into a laugh and extended a glass of orange juice towards him. Chandar got up and scooted from there like a drenched cat. Chandni slowly edged her way towards the bathroom.

"Usha Rani."

"Ji."

"You should drink this orange juice, you have a great need for it. Look how you are drooping."

"Me?"

"Yes, you're ageing. Arre, your hair is already graying at twenty-three? You're always pestering me, why don't you look at yourself in the mirror? You look so haggard."

The glass of juice slipped from Usha Rani's hand.

11

"A face like Bhagwan's, and the temperament of a devil."

Chandni was passing remarks on Barre Sarkar's picture and was very pleased with herself. Then, feeling lighthearted, she took the pen clipped on to her neckline, wrote 'devil' on the picture, and was busy drawing horns when suddenly all hell broke loose.

"Hai Ram!" When Chandni turned around she felt Masi's resounding slap with such force that stars danced before her eyes.

"You wretch! Treacherous creature! Thief!" A storm of Masi's wallops and slaps rained down on her. "You make a hole in the very plate you eat from! Vile creature, born of a harlot!"

Chandni's screams brought everyone rushing. When she tried to wipe the picture with her dupatta, Masi pushed her away violently and stood in front of it like a police inspector who has found the body.

"Look at this, look at the misdeeds of your beloved girl!" she said, shoving the picture in Chandar's face.

"You...you wrote this?"

"Chandarji..." Chandni stammered fearfully.

"Yes, yes, go ahead, say you didn't write it, you daughter of a whore." The minute she saw Barre Sarkar emerging from the library, Masi let go of Chandni and rushed towards him.

"I tell you, dump this feckless creature in an orphanage. Look... just look!" Masi burst into tears.

"Wonderful!" Barre Sarkar smiled generously. He was tired of being worshipped by the entire household. Instead of feeling angry with Chandni, he found a kind of sweetness in her mischievousness. "But Masi, if someone has a particular idea about me what is there to feel bad about?" and he walked way laughing.

"A curse on her ideas! This base-born creature!"

"Chandarji, it was...it was just a joke."

"Do you have the kind of relationship with him that you can make such jokes?" Chandar shouted.

"Chandarji, I beg of you, I made a mistake, I fall at your feet."

"It won't do to beg me and fall at my feet. Go and ask for forgiveness from the one you've insulted." Chandar pushed her away roughly.

"Oh...no..." Chandni winced.

"So you won't ask for forgiveness? I swear, you'll get such a beating that..." Chandar growled angrily.

"Then beat me."

"Get away from me! And if you ever try to talk to me in future you'll be in trouble."

"All right, I'll ask forgiveness, let's go."

"Why should I go?" Chandar settled down on the easy chair.

"Hai, so should I go alone?" Chandni said.

"Will someone devour you if you go alone?"

"But... I..." Chandni couldn't proceed. "Pimo Rani."

"No, my dear, I don't want to get involved in this. Anyway, I have to go to class."

"Hey Bhagwan! I pray to Ram that I should die this very minute. Pimoji, just come with me up to the door...my dearest Pimoji..." Chandni tried to sweet-talk her.

"All right, I'll come up to the door with you, but I'm telling you right now I will not go inside," Pimo said.

"But you wretch, why did you do this? Oh my God, calling Barre Bhaiya a devil! He cares so much about you."

"You don't know—" Chandni broke off suddenly.

"Arre, I know. He stares at you and you think he hates you. No, Chandni, he's not angry with you, he's angry with Chandar and that's because he's thinking of the family's prestige. But you'll see, he'll agree in the end. Here, go in now," she said as they reached Barre Sarkar's door.

"Pimo, you come too..."

"I'm not listening."

"But wait...just see what he is doing."

"He's reading—a book," Pimo said, peeping in.

"What is it?" They heard Barre Sarkar ask.

"She...Chandni...Barre Bhaiya..." Pimo was trapped.

"Yes?"

"She...she wants to say she's sorry."

"Oh?" Barre Sarkar could not control the beating of his heart. "Let her come in," he said, wiping the sweat from his forehead.

"You come too, Rani," Chandni grabbed Pimo's shirt.

"Parmila, tell Durga to bring tea," Barre Sarkar ordered. Pimo extricated herself from Chandni's grip and ran off.

Chandni tried to make her escape as well, but then, finding it impossible to exit, entered the room gingerly. Barre Sarkar was sitting at his desk with his back to her. She turned to go.

"So you've come to say you're sorry?" He turned around but kept his eyes on the book in his hands. Chandni felt encouraged.

"Come, sit down."

She came forward timidly and rested her body against the chair as if she was a bird ready to fly off at the slightest disturbance.

"So what are the sins you have come to ask forgiveness for?"

"Ji." Her lifeless voice caught in her throat.

"Yes." He sighed. "I'm being punished for the sins I committed in my previous life," he added, as if speaking to himself.

"I made a mistake, I want to ask your forgiveness," she said and turned to leave.

"But I haven't forgiven you yet," he smiled roguishly. "Sit."

But Chandni remained standing.

"No one answers my question," he muttered.

"Ji?" Chandni didn't understand what was happening. An unknown fear seemed to be suffocating her. She looked at him questioningly.

"When you look at me like this my head begins to explode." There were evil spirits raising their heads in his gaze.

Chandni lowered her eyes, Barre Sarkar broke into a laugh.

"This is even worse," he mumbled.

"Should I go?"

"But answer my questions first." He got up from his chair.

"Me?"

"Yes, you—do you want to make a spectacle of me?" Suddenly he looked very angry.

Chandni hastily dropped her eyes.

"This is even more cruel," Barre Sarkar protested.

"Shall I...shall I go?"

"First answer my questions! What has happened to me?" He gripped his head between his hands. "I'll go mad."

Chandni tried to run out quickly.

"Wait." He leapt up and grabbed her arm. The moment he touched her it was if explosives had been detonated in the air, a silent blast took place, and Barre Sarkar's body began to shake. The veins in his neck became taut, a river of sweat poured from him. Imploring, he placed her hand on his heart. It seemed as if a monster was jumping in his bosom. Suddenly he was no longer conscious of what he was doing. Like a wild animal he tore off her clothes, ripped them to shreds. A stifled scream emerged from Chandni's mouth and countless snakes began to sting her lips.

There was a loud clanging noise as the aarti salver shattered the stillness of the air.

"You harlot, you witch! May you die!" Masi clawed her own throat with both hands as if there was something stuck in it. Suddenly she stumbled and hit the chair. Her face turned blue, as though stung by a snake, her expression became deathly and she collapsed on the floor.

Hearing the crashing of the salver and Chandni's screams the entire household rushed to the scene.

"Doctor, for Bhagwan's sake, call the doctor..." Usha placed her mother's head in her lap and began to sob loudly.

Pimo, stunned by the sight of Chandni glued to the wall in this awful condition, quickly pulled off a blanket from the bed and threw it over her, and Chandni darted from the room.

Chandar sprinkled water on Masi's face.

"No!" Barre Sarkar screamed loudly, and then seeing everyone staring at him in surprise, recovered quickly, "I will call right away."

While he was dialling the number he realised that if Masi survived, the veneer he had covered himself with would be stripped and he would never be able to live with this dishonour.

"Yes," the doctor was saying on the phone, "Hello."

But Barre Sarkar looked around him guiltily like a criminal and put the phone down.

Masi was a longtime heart patient. It was not necessary for Barre Sarkar to have burdened his conscience. Even if the doctor had been informed, she would have died before he arrived.

Masi wanted to say many things before she died, but she had lost her voice. She tried to place Usha's hand in his, but he pretended not to notice, just sat next to her and kept weeping. Who knows whether he was crying for Masi, or was mourning an end slowly creeping up to his own existence! Everyone believed Masi had beaten up Chandni in anger and subsequently suffered a brain haemorrhage.

Barre Sarkar did not feel the need to confirm this and Chandni could not bring herself to speak.

Silence hung over the house for many months. Barre Sarkar isolated himself completely. Staying in his room by himself, lost in a world of his own thoughts, he felt more disoriented than ever. As for Chandni, she made every effort to keep out of his way.

The responsibility for the entire household now fell upon Usha Rani. She acquired the demeanour of a housewife, a wife whom the husband has forgotten about after depositing her somewhere with all the goods and chattels of his household.

The season was abuzz with new life, the forest was ablaze with tesu blossoms, Barre Sarkar looked somewhat agitated, but the atmosphere was calm.

Chandni was carelessly floating down the stairs like a butterfly. Today, feeling tired of his seclusion, Barre Sarkar had finally emerged from his room and was at the piano in the lounge, slowly strumming the keys. The moment he saw her the embers that had lain low all these months stirred suddenly and his fingers played feverishly. Startled, Chandni tried to make a hasty retreat.

"Listen!" His voice sizzled like the hissing of a snake.

The hair on her body stood on end and she was rooted to the ground.

"Come here."

Two black cobras emerged from his eyes and wrapped themselves around her body. Pulled by some unknown power, she advanced slowly towards him. The air was still, the surrounding atmosphere motionless. Barre Sarkar's gaze pierced her body like red-hot steel rods.

Slowly he grasped her tiny waist between his hands. Little by little his hands began to move upward. Up, further up. Her arms hung loosely by her sides, she trembled like a wounded bird. With a slight tug of his hands she fell against his chest.

Chandar came running noisily down the stairs. Suddenly the atmosphere resounded, Chandni hastily released herself from Barre Sarkar's hands and fell into Chandar's arms.

"Chandarji, Chandar…"

Barre Sarkar dropped his hands on the piano keys and put his head down on them.

Chandar was very annoyed with Chandni for seizing hold of him like this in Barre Sarkar's presence.

"Arre, arre, Barre Bhaiya is sitting over there, you silly girl."

Chandni jumped away from him and walked to the steps, her feet dragging.

"What's the matter, Barre Bhaiya?" Chandar was worried, seeing Barre Bhaiya with his head down like this. "Do you have a headache?"

"Hunh? Oh, yes."

"Uff-oh! You read all day, that's why. I'll fix it right away."

"Chandni," he called her from the bottom of the stairs.

"What is it, Chandarji?" Chandni replied tonelessly.

"Could you bring the bottle of almond oil from Didi's room," he said. "Barre Bhaiya, lie back on the chair comfortably." Settling him in the chair he began to untie his shoelaces.

When Chandni appeared with the bottle of oil he said, "Would you put a little oil on Bhaiya's hair," and began massageing Bhaiya's feet.

"I? Chandarji?"

"Yes."

"I have work to do...you...why don't you do it?" She became tearful.

"Arre, I have to go for tennis practice later, my hands will become oily and the racket will slip from my fingers."

"Wash your hands before you go."

"Don't talk nonsense. You won't faint if you put oil in his hair."

Although he was afraid of confronting Chandni in private, in public he always showed his bravado.

"It's all right, Chandar, it will go away in a short while," Barre Sarkar moaned as if in pain.

"Arre wah, how can it go away by itself? Chandni!"

Unnerved by the roughness in his voice, Chandni started applying oil to Barre Sarkar's hair. He was soon enjoying her discomfort.

"Chandar, where is today's newspaper?" he asked, pushing the paper under his arm. Chandni broke into a cold sweat.

"It must be in your room."

"No, it's not there."

"Maybe it's on the veranda. Should I bring it?"

"Please."

"And I also have to pay for the racket."

"The wallet is at my bedside."

"I'll be back in a minute." Chandar bounded up the stairs.

"Chandarji," Chandni's voice stuck in her throat.

A sneer spread over Barre Sarkar's face, his nostrils flared, the veins in his neck throbbed. Pretending to scratch his neck he groped for Chandni's fingers. Terrified, Chandni pulled her hand back.

Her eyes were pinned to the staircase, waiting for that fool Chandar, wondering when he would bring the newspaper and she would be free to leave. If only she could have spoken when Barre Sarkar hid the paper under his arm—but how could she muster such courage? In the meantime Barre Sarkar was continuing to play with her fingers.

Chandni's prayers were answered. Usha Rani was returning from the kitchen. If someone else did Barre Sarkar's work, it was an infringement of her rights. She came in quietly and moving Chandni aside, began to pat Sarkar's head. Suddenly Barre Bhaiya opened his eyes and peacocks danced joyfully in his heart. He again tried to stroke her hands. When he felt a return pressure, responding to his touch, he was intoxicated. Usha blossomed like a fragrant flower. Finding no resistance, she surrendered her trembling fingers to his. Barre Sarkar gently dug his nails into her palm. Quivering with happiness, Usha closed her eyes. Emboldened, he placed her hand on his cheek. With only a slight tug, Usha Rani fell into his lap like ripe fruit.

The heavens seemed to have fallen on Barre Sarkar! He shoved Usha aside and stood up quickly. Her support gone, Usha Rani fell with a thud on the floor. Because of the sudden interruption in her enjoyment she couldn't grasp the situation fully and stared wide-eyed at the anger blazing in Sarkar's eyes. She trembled in fear.

"Oh. I see." She understood immediately what had happened and shook her head.

"What do you see? You understand nothing. If you had the ability to understand then…"

"Then what?"

"Then…then it wouldn't be necessary to say…that…that…Uff-oh!"

He melted at the sight of the tears flowing down Usha's face.

"You don't like anything I do?"

"But why are you always pestering me? Why don't you do other things in the house?"

"My touching you displeased you so much, but she…she."

"Who?" Barre Sarkar roared.

"You know who! You held my hand because you thought it was hers!"

Usha Rani couldn't tolerate this humiliation and began to sob uncontrollably.

"Stop this nonsense! You idiot…do you…do you want to dishonour my name? You…" He shook her violently by the shoulders. Weeping hysterically she fell at his feet.

"Please don't do this, for Bhagwan's sake, I'll die, please don't turn me away like this."

"Usha Rani, it's better that you die rather than insult the name of women like this. For Bhagwan's sake, don't force me."

"You'll regret this, what you are doing is so unfair."

Suddenly he began to feel sorry for Usha Rani.

"Why should you care, why do you care so much about me?"

"Because…because…you know yourself that one cannot help something like this."

"Oh! Please stop aggravating me…go now."

"I…"

"Go, I say!"

Usha Rani stifled her sobs and turned away swiftly.

"Usha…Usha…for my sake."

Usha halted in her tracks like a wounded deer.

"You know, you're so silly…I was joking and you started crying!" he said, gently touching her chin. Usha gaped at him like a fool.

"Chandar made her put oil in my hair, I couldn't refuse. Then you came and I knew immediately it was you. I don't know what came over me but just to tease you…I was joking, and when you fell I became nervous…just think…I thought you would pull your hand away."

"Oh." That this was all her fault made Usha turn red.

"If you were offended, please forgive me, I made a mistake."

"But…but you don't like me to do anything for you."

"No, I don't like it at all. My blood boils when I see you working. What are all these servants for? It's just that when you're stubborn I lose my temper and say things I don't mean. Afterwards, I feel sorry. Can you forgive me?"

"Arre, you've scraped your elbow. I'm a very bad person."

"No…No, I'm not hurt."

Poor Usha had no experience of lovers, and thought in her heart that this was how they behaved. She continued to smile. Chandar came in just then.

"I couldn't find the newspaper anywhere. Arre, it's right here."

When Barre Sarkar had got up in panic the paper slipped from under his arm and fell on the floor. "You always dash up the stairs in such a hurry, I called after you but you didn't hear me."

Chandar, embarrassed, turned to leave.

"Arre, Chandar, come here," Barre Sarkar said, "pick up the paper and bring it with you." After that he had a long discussion with Chandar on the subject of sports.

Silently cursing Chandar and heaving a sigh, Usha left. She had been afforded a small chance, a reasonably hopeful love scene had been in progress and this wretch had to show up just then. The occasion lost its momentum. But that was all right, for when her dreams were woven tonight the feel of his hands, the brief interlude in his embrace, the touch of his fingers on her chin—all of this would come to life and light up her solitude.

Instead of gradually diminishing because of one setback after another, Sarkar's ardour for Chandni began to assume strange forms. If he had been an ordinary mortal circumstances might not have taken such a delicate turn. He would have fallen in love with Usha or developed an intense dislike for women, or he would have taken an oath to remain celibate for the rest of his life. But he was slowly losing self-control, his obsession was growing. At night he would pace unshod on the roof in the cold air. If he succeeded in finally falling asleep the ghouls and spirits that inhabited his thoughts would find release and start creating a commotion. He would have no strength left then and his unconscious would become its own master. Sometimes, when he woke up, he would realise that he had walked to Chandni's room and was standing at her threshold, banging his head on her door, weeping uncontrollably. When he came to he would flee from there, weak with feelings of shame and humiliation. In the silence of the night he would wander deep into the woods. He was now terrified of falling asleep as well because once, while sleepwalking, he found himself on the turret leading to a window in Chandni's room. Only a narrow ledge connected it to the window. His desire for Chandni was pulling him towards her like a magnet. His weakness and fear had become subservient to his sixth sense, an unseen ghostly power was the only thing that was wide awake.

A heart-rending scream pierced the silence, dashed against the hills and recoiled, a star fell and disappeared, and Barre Sarkar was awakened by a loud explosion. He saw that he had arrived at the window. His hand was bleeding profusely from having smashed the glass. All at once his sixth sense abandoned him. When his gaze travelled to the khud below the whole world began to rock. Everyone wants to live, and right now Barre Sarkar was not a god but an ordinary, frightened human being. He clung to the wall and closed his eyes.

Chandni's continuous screaming woke everyone up.

"There...he..." Chandni kept pointing to the window like someone who had lost her mind. "Barre Sarkar...Barre Sarkar..." And she collapsed in Chandar's arms. Handing her over to Pimo, Chandar rushed to the window. Usha Didi was already there.

"Who was it?" Chandar tried to open the window.

"No...no one." Usha screamed and grabbed the window casement with both hands.

"Let me see, please. If someone was there, he can't have got away that quickly."

"No!" She pushed Chandar away. She knew that if Barre Sarkar's secret was revealed he would not be able to live. Before she closed the window she had seen his bloody hand with his ring and knew it was him. She had nursed suspicions for a while now—how long can the beloved conceal what is in his heart from his mad lover! But she was not his lover, she was his devotee.

"No, Chandar, if it's a thief he will cut your throat!" Pimo screamed.

If he slips he will die, Usha thought, gritting her teeth, but at least his honour will not be sullied. She was trembling violently, in fearful expectation of the accident that was about to happen. She listened closely in the silence for the sound of Barre Sarkar's footsteps as he slowly drew back. A stone fell and kept banging against the wall all the way down into the khud. Usha stifled a sob.

"There is someone out there, let me see please." Chandar tried to move her out of the way but she tensed and screamed with such force that he withdrew nervously.

"Chandar Bhaiya, why do you want to put your life in danger?" Pimo was able to avert a very delicate situation with her characteristic innocence. "Usha Didi, don't let him look."

"Everyone return to your rooms. Pimo, take Chandni to my room."

"Should I sleep there as well?"

"Yes, you sleep with her and I'll sleep here."

"No, Usha Didi, what if he returns?"

"No, my dear, the thief will not come again," Usha said tonelessly.

"Chandni, did you see the thief with your own eyes?" Pimo asked.

"It wasn't a thief…it was…" Chandni stopped in midsentence.

"Not a thief? Then who was it?"

"Nobody," Chandni said annoyingly.

"Then why did you scream?"

"It was a dream, I got frightened."

"But…who broke the glass on the window?"

"Stop pestering me!" Chandni burst into tears.

"Arre wah, I'm just asking." Pimo's face fell.

"Don't ask, just go to sleep, Pimo Rani," Chandni said affectionately.

"Chandni," Pimo asked before falling asleep.

"Yes?"

"You called out to Barre Bhaiya."

"I did? No, of course not."

"Yes, when I woke up you were screaming, 'Barre Sarkar, Barre Sarkar!" Pimo imitated her.

"Really? I don't remember."

"But he must sleep very soundly, he didn't get up."

"Hunh." Chandni covered her face with her dupatta. How could she tell Pimo? But there would never be a better time. She sat up.

"Pimo."

"Yes."

"Will you believe what I say?"

"Yes, why not?"

"If I swear on Chandarji's life, will you believe me?"

"Yes, what is it?"

"That glass…" She could say no more, Usha was standing in the doorway. By the light of the candle she saw that there were flames blazing in her eyes.

"So what were you saying?" Pimo hadn't seen Usha.

"If you want to talk rubbish at two in the night you can both get out of here," Usha scolded.

"But Usha Didi, in Chandni's room there's a…"

"Yes, go there. It'll be great if the thief throttles you both. Tell me, how could Chandni see anybody in the dark, and who could it be? The khud is full of thieves and crooks."

"But how did the thief climb up?" Pimo cross-examined.

"I don't know how he climbed up! We'll find out in the morning. Everyone go to sleep now without another word, understand?"

She retrieved the first aid box from the cupboard and left, locking the door behind her so that Pimo couldn't pursue her out of curiosity.

"Who's injured?" Pimo asked.

"Shush…" Chandni turned on her side.

"One would think Usha Didi is related to the thief, she's defending him so much!"

"Go to sleep, Rani," Chandni begged.

"You know what?" Pimo suddenly jumped up.

"What?"

"It must be Usha Didi's sweetheart! He must have come to declare his love for her but ended up in the wrong room."

Despite her apprehensive mood Chandni burst out laughing. "Come now, you silly girl."

"Really, that must be it, that's why she's constantly coming to his defence. She herself leaned out of the window and started scolding Chandro Bhaiya when he tried to take a look. If he had done so her sweetheart would have been caught."

"Pimo, if you don't stop talking rubbish I will strike my own head," Chandni warned angrily and Pimo finally stopped talking.

She fell asleep at last but Chandni remained awake, staring at the ceiling. She was afraid to close her eyes. Again and again they travelled to the dimly-lit windows, as if a stranger was standing next to each one and she felt that the minute she closed her eyes, one of them would come and land on her chest. Her helplessness drove her to tears and also made her angry. Why had she been born, wretch that she was? Would the world have ended if she hadn't been?

Usha ran with the first aid box first to Chandni's room. Her heart beating violently, she opened the window and flashed a torchlight; there was no one there. He hadn't fallen for if he had she would have heard him falling. Then she saw that there were bloodstains on the wall he had leaned against. She heaved a sigh of relief. This meant he had reached the turret safely.

She rushed to his room. As she entered she found him rummaging through a drawer in the closet. When he turned at the sound of her footsteps she saw that he had a pistol in his hand. Usha acted as though she had seen nothing. She put the box gently on the table, sat on the stool nearby and calmly took out spirit, cotton and bandages.

"Where are the scissors?" Usha opened a drawer and retrieved a pair of scissors.

"You can sit here on the bed," she said casually.

The blood had congealed in Barre Sarkar's eyes, his cheeks had sunk in, he looked as if he had been ill for a long time. There were thorny bushes on the turret which is why his clothes were in shreds. He advanced towards Usha with the gun and stared wildly at her. The muzzle of the pistol rested close to her temple but she neither trembled nor experienced fear. She wasn't afraid of dying, it was as if in the midst of life's awful bitterness death had lost its lustre.

Their eyes met and for a few minutes they exchanged glances. Barre Sarkar's eyes were filled with hate, loathing and unfulfilled longing, but in Usha's eyes there was the sweetness of abiding love, tenderness and affection.

Barre Sarkar's eyes fell! The pistol slipped from his hands and in the next instant he dropped his head in Usha's lap and began to sob like a child.

"Usha Rani, save me...save me, Usha, marry me, now, this moment... Usha...or else...or else I will go mad, my head will explode. Usha save me!"

For one second Usha recoiled, as if someone had plunged a knife all the way into her heart. She wanted to ask:

Do you really hate me so much? Have I committed such a great sin by loving you that I can atone for it in no other way? But at this time there's neither love nor hate for you in my heart, just a void! Perhaps because I have partaken of your salt all my life, it now inhabits every vein in my body.

But she said nothing. She just looked at him with tired eyes and a poisonous smile spread over her face. Quietly she lowered her head and concentrated on bandaging his hand. When she finished, she put everything back again neatly in the box and, closing the door behind her, left.

Usha spent that night pacing the veranda. How solitary her fate! How lonely her world! Especially after Masi's death she felt she was a calf roaming around without its mother. She hadn't learnt to place any kind of blame on Barre Sarkar, had always regarded him above reproach.

The heavens are testing him. The gods are displeased with him because he is greater than they are, he is superior to the ordinary worms crawling on earth. That is why Chandni has been sent by them in the form of a beguiling woman to destroy him. In truth he was not so low as to cast a lustful eye on a mere child. All the satanic powers had collectively taken the form of an unknown girl and were enticing him. He alone had the ability to silently suffer the torment of earlier lives. If it were someone else he would have fulfilled his desire and then destroyed the girl who had been sent to destroy him. The sun god is special because he blesses the particles of dust with heat, he doesn't pick up the dust and cover his face with it. That is why Barre Sarkar is putting his life on the line, to battle what the fates have in store for him. And Usha's place is at his feet. He is her venerated god, her master. Who knows what sins she had committed in the previous life to have been rewarded with this life-threatening love for him. His rejection of her is her honour. Who knows which form the god takes is real and which disguise he has assumed to destroy Chandni. But he doesn't love anyone! If he does, then it's this devotee of his that he loves! If he is suffering from an illness, is it not her duty to sacrifice her life in order to save him?

When her legs became heavy with all the pacing and her mind wearied with all the thinking, then Usha picked up a book of Meera's bhajans and found an echo of her pain in them. Her being was finally at peace.

Girdhar Gopal is mine
No one else.

She kept reading it in a low voice, swaying with the words. The entire world was asleep, a woman was burning the lamp of her sorrows in her heart, but the night was still dark.

She stopped suddenly as a thought crossed her mind. Without worrying about taking someone along, she draped herself in a shawl and started walking quickly towards Sarna Devi's shrine. She did not feel the darkness of the dense woods. Tigers had been seen here, snakes and scorpions were known to frequent the dark areas, but Usha Devi's love had illuminated the entire universe and the path shone like the Milky Way. In the distance somewhere jackals were howling, owls were hooting in accompaniment, but Usha Devi kept walking, intoxicated like Sati Savitri with the desire to safeguard her beloved.

12

Chandni screamed as if it wasn't Chandar she had bumped into in the gallery but an evil spirit.

She couldn't sleep in Usha's room. All around her the new surroundings took on strange and terrifying shapes to frighten her. The doors and windows had been bolted from the inside but her gaze still strayed towards them. She tried very hard to distract herself, but no sooner had she stopped feeling tense about the doors and windows than she would feel that the wall was slowly splitting into two, dark shadows were emerging from within and would seize her any second.

She was afraid of falling asleep. She got up, splashed some cold water on her face, changed her clothes and came out. The long corridor was isolated. In the bluish late-night light shadows leapt from all sides to attack her. Taking quick strides she came to the end of the corridor and that was where she bumped into Chandar and screamed.

"Arre wah, you silly girl, you're scared of me now?" Startled, Chandar laughed at her.

"Chandarji…hai, I will die." She placed her head on his chest and began to sob violently.

"You've gone mad. I thought I heard someone opening the front gate and I came to see if it was you."

"Chandar, I'm afraid, the walls of the house scare me, they will devour me. Take me away from here or I will suffocate."

"What kind of talk is this, Chandni?"

"If you don't take me away, I'll go alone." Angered, she pushed Chandar aside.

"But what's the reason for this? How cold your hands are." Chandar blew on them, holding them in his own.

"Reason? I can't tell you the reason. All I can say is that if you don't take me away from here this very minute you will see my corpse tomorrow."

"Chandni, don't talk like that. I'll die with you." Chandar pulled her into his arms.

"But I don't want to die! I'm alive in the hope that one day you will put sindhur in my hair. Then I will put my head on your chest and die. Take me away from here, Chandar, don't let me die."

"Who is killing you? Let me take you to the doctor tomorrow."

"The doctor doesn't have the cure for my ailments."

"But—"

"No ifs and buts, or you'll regret this. Take me far away from here and then I will tell you everything. If my suspicions are unfounded, you can come back."

"You won't tell me here?"

"I'll tell you on the way."

"But let's wait until the morning."

"No, I may not have the strength to stay alive until then."

"All right. Here, take the key, put on your coat and sit in the car. I'll bring my coat."

She took the key, returned to her room and put on her coat. A glance at the sleeping Pimo brought tears to her eyes. She gently kissed her head, came down and got into the car to wait for Chandar.

"You took so long," Chandni said, playfully slapping the key in his hand when he came. The burden weighing on her heart was already feeling lighter. Chandar didn't reply and quickly started the car. Suddenly a pedestrian in black clothes appeared in front of them, but instead of slowing down Chandar accelerated. Chandni screamed and clung to him as the man barely escaped being run over.

"You're angry, aren't you, Chandarji," Chandni said, hugging his arm. She didn't know where to start. Looking serious, Chandar was staring ahead at the road. His face was hidden by his hat and the upturned coat collar, but there was a strange kind of tension in the air.

"Chandarji, are you angry?" she touched his hand anxiously. "Are you?"

"No." Chandar's voice sounded gravelly.

Chandni stammered out the whole story, one incident at a time. Chandar didn't seem at all furious and Chandni felt encouraged. The speed of the car increased.

"I swear on my life, Chandar, Masi saw everything with her own eyes, that was why she had a haemorrhage, she was so angry. If she hadn't died, the secret would have come out. Usha Didi also knows everything. You and Pimo are the only ones who are so innocent you know nothing. Munshiji was the first to figure it out. The wretch taunted me. I tricked him: the young one is useless, everything is in the hands of the older brother, he is the master of everything. Hunh! The very sight of his face makes me sick. What a demon! And what a saintly air he puts on! I would die rather than even spit on his life, my stupid fool is good enough for me."

Chandni draped her arms around his neck. "I don't want a raja, Chandar, I'm yours and will always be yours. Whether you marry me or keep me as your servant, in this life I am already yours."

A tremor passed through Chandar's body and he lowered his head. Agitated, he accelerated.

Suddenly Chandni was gripped by fear. Why doesn't Chandar say something? He's angry! He adores Barre Sarkar, he worships him— he hasn't lost his mind because of all this talk, has he?

"Chandarji, you don't believe me? Please don't drive so fast. Look at me, please," she implored, pulling Chandar's face toward her.

Then Chandni's eyes opened wide, fear rendered her speechless. Like a wounded pigeon she tried to open the door and jump out, but Barre Sarkar broke into a savage laugh and, grabbing her waist, pulled her in roughly.

13

Wearing his coat, muffler wrapped around his ears, Chandar arrived in the garage and was thunderstruck. There was no sign of the car. The door of the other garage was locked. Puzzled, he came out, wondering if Chandni had left without him. He was rushing to get the key when suddenly Usha Didi, covered with dust and dirt, stumbled in through the gate.

"Arre, Usha Didi! Where have you been?"

"He...he has left!"

"Who?"

"He...Barre Sarkar has taken Chandni."

"Oh, well in that case there's nothing to worry about, but—"

"You fool! Don't stand there staring, go and get the other car out! Bhagwan only knows what is about to happen today. Hurry up, Chandar." She pushed him towards the garage.

"What's the matter, Sarkar?" Some of the servants gathered.

"Keys to the car!"

"I have them," the chauffeur said and quickly went towards his room to bring them.

"Hurry up—no, you stay here," Usha took the keys from the chauffeur and dragged Chandar. "Hurry up, Chandar, hai Ram, if something happens to them...He...he..." Usha couldn't bring herself to say anything. She covered her face with her hands and started sobbing.

"Usha Didi." Chandar became very worried.

"Drive faster, Chandar..."

"I am, Didi, why are you so scared?"

"Go fast, my brother."

"How can I go any faster? A winding road, rocky terrain on one side and steep ravines on the other. Don't you see the boulders? But Usha Didi, where has Bhaiya gone at this time of night?"

"You'll find out, you'll find out everything. Just drive!"

"Usha Didi?"

"Yes."

"Is Bhaiya angry with me?"

"What?"

"He is upset that Chandni and I..."

"You and Chandni! Yes, yes, why shouldn't he be angry? The wretch, a poisonous weed, she's become a real nuisance for everyone."

"But Didi..."

"If you had been in his place and your younger brother who was dearer to you than your own life did something as low as this, would you have patted his head in approval?"

"Am I committing a sin?"

"He loves you so much. If you make a mistake doesn't he have the right to—"

"But if he had talked to me I would have given him an explanation."

"But why would he talk to you about such things?"

"Didi, if he does something...he won't treat Chandni badly, will he?" Chandar suddenly became fearful.

"Chandar, if you want Chandni and your Bhaiya to be safe don't waste time talking. Today he will take his own life and hers. The witch, how she has ensnared him in her magic!"

"Why do you keep reprimanding her? It's my fault too, I should also be punished."

"You too will receive a punishment that you will remember for many lifetimes. You planted such a poisonous seed in the house that you will not be let off lightly."

"Is he threatening her life?"

"If she doesn't listen to him today then both his life and hers are in danger."

"But who is he to make or destroy my life! I can obey his every command but he will have to listen to me where Chandni is concerned."

"So will there be bloodshed between brothers because of this harlot? Hai Ram, Chandar!" She still couldn't bring herself to speak the truth. But there was no need to tell Chandar anything. Sarna Devi was going to grant Usha's wish today, everything was going to be all right.

In the distance they spotted the car standing at a bend in the road. Chandar pressed the accelerator and the car jumped forward. When they came closer they saw that the headlights were on, but the car was empty.

14

It became so difficult to manage the steering wheel as Chandni was scratching and biting like an angry cat. Unable to continue, Barre

Sarkar stopped the car. The moment it slowed down, she slipped out
of his grasp and, opening the door, fell on the road. Then, in the next
instant, she got up and began to run wildly.

Seeing her running towards the river with the bamboo bridge
he leapt after her but, making a detour, she started clambering up
the rocks. Her shoe fell off somewhere and her dupatta flew off. He
caught up with her several times, but she was able to free herself from
him. Finally there was only one recourse left; she could either jump
into the river or submit to Barre Sarkar. She ran towards the water,
but the rocks were slippery and she kept losing her footing. And then,
when she was about to get up, she saw that Barre Sarkar was right in
front of her. She made an effort to stand but he grabbed her, seized
her foot with his hand and tightened his grip.

Clutching her foot he was sobbing and kissing it wildly. "Chandni,
I can't live without you, have pity, I'll go mad, Chandni."

A huge storm of hate and anger rose in Chandni's heart, she bent
down and picked up a heavy stone to crush the head of the snake, but
suddenly saw Chandar climbing up the rock. She felt an immense
wave of relief and dropped the stone. Covering her face with her
hands she began to cry. Finally Chandar had seen her plight.

"If you have decided then that's all right, but don't forget, my hands
will be tainted with Chandar's blood," Barre Sarkar was babbling on
and on. He was not at all aware of Chandar's presence.

"Are you listening to what your brother is saying, Chandarji, the
brother who is like your father? Come and see for yourself."

"Bhaiya!" Chandar called out and started scrambling up hastily.

Suddenly it was as if all the strength in Barre Sarkar's body seeped
out. His grip loosened and sweat drenched his body. Like a beaten
dog he cowered in a corner. As he raised his head the demon that had
been baring its teeth a few minutes earlier disappeared. In its place
was the brother like a father, the old gentleness in the eyes, the same
seriousness, the same tenderness of tone. Barre Sarkar, who was a
humble human being, and a magnificent fraud.

"Have pity, Chandni, have mercy on me. If you want the family
wealth you can have it, my share and Pimo's well, but for Bhagwan's

sake give up Chandar. I promised my mother on her deathbed that I would take care of Chandar, and if I have to give up my life to do that I will feel I have done my duty."

All colour drained from Chandni's face, her throat was parched and her tongue became glued to the roof of her mouth. Eyes wide open, she stared in horror at this masquerader.

"Bhaiya, what are you saying?" Chandar sounded remorseful.

"I'm begging Chandni for your life. My brother, how young you were—our mother placed your hand in mine and said, 'Promise me that you will look out for Chandar.' If Maa's soul is troubled what reason will I have to live then?" Barre Sarkar was being melodramatic.

All at once Chandni pulled her foot from his grip and running to Chandar, grabbed his shirt.

"He is a fake, Chandarji, don't listen to him! This is all a farce, lies—just moments ago he was threatening to take your life, he is a liar, Chandarji—this villain has—"

"Chandni, have you gone mad?" Chandar said, frightened by the wild look in her eyes. He was not used to hearing such dreadful things spoken about Barre Bhaiya.

"I'm mad and you're very clever! Chandar, you absolute fool…"

"Don't talk rubbish, Chandni, or I will slap you so hard that your face will be bent out of shape…you have no control over your tongue!"

Chandni looked once at the godlike form of Barre Sarkar, then turned to look at the innocent, naive Chandar and broke into hysterical laughter.

"I'm mad and you're not mad. I'm a sinner and you are all gods. Because of me one brother is ready to kill the other, because of me the forehead of Suraj Vansh is about to be tainted." Chandni's sigh ended on a sob. Dawn was breaking, the sun was about to rise. In the far distance, on the banks of the river, the moon's visage was turning pale yellow, moonlight was taking its last breath.

Chandni bent down to pick up a pinch of dirt at Chandar's feet to put in her hair. For one moment she stood before him, looked long and hard at him, then turned around and ran towards the river. Usha Rani tried to stop her, the guard at the bridge shouted, "The bridge is falling apart," but she flashed past everyone with the swiftness of an arrow. The bridge swayed dangerously, its bamboo shafts began to split and fall into the river below.

Like a madman Barre Sarkar got to his feet and dashed after her.

"Stop her!" He panicked when he saw her walking into the jaws of death.

"What are you doing, Sarkar! It won't be able to withstand the weight of two people, stop for Bhagwan's sake!" The guard tried to grab him by the waist, Chandar tried to pin him down, but he was filled with extraordinary power. He pushed everyone aside and jumped onto the bridge.

"What are you doing, Chandni, come back!" he shouted. A bamboo shaft split under Chandni's foot, her leg fell through the gap all the way to her knee. When she tried to extricate herself, the wood began to splinter. Seeing Barre Sarkar approach, she managed to get her foot out and crossed to the other side in one big leap. She hadn't quite regained her footing when, along with Barre Sarkar, the ancient bridge, creaking and growling, plunged into the river below.

"Barre Bhaiya!" Chandar knew he couldn't swim. The current of the river swept Barre Sarkar along with the rotting remains of the bridge and surged forward—despite warnings by the guard, Chandar threw off his coat and jumped in.

Barre Sarkar wrestled with death for a week. Chandar had risked his own life and saved him. Sarkar had received several stitches in his head and on his face. The fever was slowly abating. The doctors had said that he was out of danger, but Usha Rani remained constantly at his bedside. If she became drowsy she would lean her head against the bedpost and sleep for a while. With great difficulty Pimo and Chandar forced her to eat something. She wouldn't let anyone into the room except for the doctors. Once in a while someone would come in for a few minutes but if Barre Sarkar became agitated, she immediately threw them out. No one except she and Chandni knew the truth. She didn't think Munshiji was important. She had warned Chandni sternly not to utter a word to anyone. She was not interested in anything except Barre Sarkar's life at this moment.

Chandni was badly shaken herself and could barely think, had secluded herself from Pimo and Chandar.

When Usha was satisfied that Barre Sarkar was feeling better, she began coaxing Chandni, using hints and innuendo, that the time had come to repay her debt to this family. But Chandni was not as strong as Usha Rani. The clever woman drew pictures of the splendours of heaven, provided reassurances by presenting images of a peaceful existence in the next life, lectured her on making sacrifices, but Chandni was not ready to die.

"I'll go somewhere, far away from here."

"Chandar will come after you."

"Is there nothing but death written in my fate?"

"This is not death, you silly girl! You will become eternal. If something happens to Him, will Chandar continue to love you? Will he be able to marry the woman responsible for his brother's death?"

"No...but..."

"If his brother lives he will spend his life worshipping you."

"And Chandar will love me?" Chandni said with a sob.

"Yes."

"He will worship me, he will be in pain when he thinks of me, my memory will make him sad."

"Yes."

"Then I will die."

"I know, Chandni, you're not some low-caste girl, you're the avatar of a goddess."

"Yes, I'm the avatar of a goddess, but Didi...I was so scared of falling into the river when I was on the bridge. I went there to die, but couldn't. The knife will hurt very much, and I don't even know how to use it. Didi..."

"Yes?"

"Why don't you plunge the knife into my heart or ask Chandarji to strangle me," Chandni began to weep.

"It's a sin to kill anyone." Usha valued her own life.

"But it's also a sin to kill oneself."

"Killing yourself is a sin, but sacrificing yourself is a good deed of the highest order, Chandni. I have a nectar which will make you fall into a deep and satisfying sleep."

"And then?"

"Then you will never wake up."

"Who gave you this nectar, Didi?"

"Sarna Mayya. After Mataji passed away I was very depressed and unhappy, I thought it's better that I join her rather than be alone like this. All my sorrows will cease," Usha Rani made up a story.

"But you didn't drink the nectar?"

"No. That very night Mataji appeared in my dream and said, 'It is your duty to serve my Barre Sarkar. Your life and your death are at his feet.'"

"All right Didi, tell me something."

"What?"

"If I drink this nectar will I go to my mother?"

"When you die you will meet everyone."

"Then give me the nectar. I will go to my mother, I will place my head in her lap and close my eyes and ask her, 'Ma, what sin did I commit that you abandoned me on a rubbish heap? Clasp me to your breast.' But Didi, how will I recognize her? I've never seen her."

"You can recognize everyone when you meet them after death." Usha retrieved a tiny vial from her purse.

"But who knows, maybe my mother and father are still alive and I will be wandering alone."

"If they were alive, why would they have abandoned you and disappeared?"

"No, they couldn't have abandoned me. I'm sure I got lost and some thug or robber left me there. They would have wept and wept hopelessly. Who knows, maybe they're still looking for me. Didi Rani, can we look for them? Maybe I also have brothers and they are looking all over the world for me. Hai Didi, my heart says I have a brother somewhere, he doesn't know that his unfortunate sister is living somewhere, crying over her fate." Chandni's weeping turned into loud sobs.

Usha got tired of her rambling and left. Chandni clutched the vial in her fist and continued to weep silently. Hearing Chandar's voice, she felt her heart take a plunge. He was looking for her. His call awakened her desire to live. Oh, the days they had spent together, days of love, life's melodious moments that were so far from death, days that had become a dream and had vanished. Chandar called out her name again, then left. She crouched in a corner of the gallery. The entire household was sleeping peacefully, she was the only one awake.

Why is it that one person suffers so much but no one is aware of the pain?

At any other time she would have started screaming if she so much as saw Barre Sarkar's shadow. But now when she saw him slowly approaching the gallery, her heart did not beat violently nor did she cry out. He came closer and stood before her like a criminal, his arms dangling by his sides. Suddenly Chandni became aware of her own power. She was noble, was going to make a sacrifice. She had the nectar of eternal life in her hand. She had nothing to do with anyone, either with Barre Sarkar's love or Chandar's hate, she had nothing to do with anyone anymore.

"Do you love me?" she asked boldly.

"Yes." Barre Sarkar's voice rustled like the air sweeping through the cremation ground. His whole body began to shake. Closing his eyes, he leaned against the wall.

"Will you promise me?" she said, grinding her teeth.

"Yes." He held his head between his hands.

"So do it." Chandni's voice was flat and expressionless.

"You...you..." Barre Sarkar starting tearing at his throat with both hands.

"Yes, I've decided."

He touched her shoulder cautiously, perhaps to see whether she was real or a vision. From her shoulder his hand travelled up to her wet cheek. He flinched as if he had placed it on live coals.

"You...you...you're playing a game with me." He looked at Chandni in fear. The same Chandni who used to cringe and recoil when face to face with him was looking at him serenely. She opened her fist and gazed lovingly at the vial of nectar and broke into a smile. Barre Sarkar stared at her in surprise for a while, then pulled her close and searched for the answer to his question in her eyes. But there was nothing in them. Exhausted, he lurched forward.

Seeing him like this Chandni's heart melted. What was Barre Sarkar if not a masquerader? Filled with a strange kind of maternal feeling, she put both her icy hands on his burning temples and pulled his head down to rest against her bosom.

"Chandni." Chandar blinked like a fool as he saw this strange drama unfold. Chandni did not turn to look at him but Barre Sarkar jumped back. Seeing a reflection of the crumbling image of his superiority and piety in Chandar's eyes, he lowered his gaze in shame and began shaking like a leaf.

"Chandarji, we are getting married." Chandni took a life-threatening chance and teased Chandar. In one stroke she had changed from a naive young girl into an old woman. "Have you seen the bridegroom?"

"Have you gone mad?" Chandar shook her by the shoulders but she darted out of his grasp.

"Don't touch me, because this palace of sand will collapse in a minute if you do. Why are you staring at me like this? Why are you meddling?"

"What's happened to her? Bhaiya, you—"

"Yes, I...I am the sun." Barre Sarkar swayed as if intoxicated. "And she...she is the moonlight...did you...did you see? How the world lies when it says the sun and the moon can never unite! All this is nonsense because...because my real name is not Suraj, it's Chand...Chand."

"Bhaiya, you're not feeling well."

"I'm perfectly well...because my...my name is not Suraj any more."

Usha Rani swooped down screeching like an eagle.

"You ungrateful wretch, you shameless boy, you are insulting your older brother for this worthless girl? Look at the state he's in, how can you bear to see him in this condition? But you're bent on taking his life."

"Didi!"

"Don't say another word! What has he not done for you? He wasted his youth for you, he said until Pimo and Chandar are independent I won't sleep in peace. If it had been someone else he would have plucked you out like a fly in the milk and thrown you aside. But he never looked at you in anger, never raised his voice, and you are crossing all limits?" She supported Barre Sarkar, gently propelled him to a chair and helped him sit down.

"I...what have I done?" Chandar felt that he too, like the others, was losing his mind.

"What did you not do? You brought this witch into our house. Weren't you the one to bring her here?" Usha thought this was the only way she could keep Chandar in check. "At your insistence we raised this she-cobra, what did she ever lack? She had greater comforts than the family's real daughter, and today this shameless creature is paying everyone back by pitting brother against brother. But as long as I'm alive I won't allow this family to be destroyed, even if I have to make a sacrifice of my own blood. I, too, have eaten the salt of this house and I will not be disloyal. Nor will I permit betrayal."

"Uff-oh Didi, listen to me. I came here and saw—"

"Go away, don't call me Didi. What can someone who has no compassion for his defenceless, god-like brother do for an orphaned, helpless girl like me?" Usha broke into tears. "Everyone has complaints against him. Ask Chandni."

"I don't want to ask anyone anything," Chandar said hatefully.

"Chandarji." Chandni had never seen him look so grave. He was about to walk away when he paused.

Usha glared at her threateningly, signs of life stirred in her eyes and then began to dissolve. Wearily she dropped her head to one side.

"Yes, Chandarji, ask me—but you're still very young, you haven't learnt to be scorched by love yet continue to smile. What will you understand?"

"You...Barre Bhaiya..." His voice wobbled.

"Yes, who doesn't love the nectar of life?" She opened her fist and kissed the tiny vial.

"Then why did you keep me in the dark for so long?"

"Life itself is a deception, all I know is that everyone will meet after the sweet slumber of death, then I will sleep...I'm so tired."

"And you fooled me by saying how scared you were of him, that he hated you, wanted to kill you." Chandar's voice was filled with bitterness.

"Does anyone know the secrets of love and hate? No one can erase what destiny has in store for us. Nobody has any control over what is fated to happen."

"Don't use fate and destiny as an excuse. Why don't you admit you wanted to be a queen and your wish has now been fulfilled. I...I am a fool, of course...a coward, afraid of everyone. Do you think anyone will die because of you?" The blood racing in Chandar's veins was passionate and proud.

"You're right, I want to be a queen, so I'll become a queen before morning. And yes, you're a fool and a coward. You cower in the presence of Barre Sarkar. You're not fit to be the dust at his feet, and I would be insane to reject the sun god and go with the moon that shines in his shadow. He, he is a god, an exceptional man, and you? You're nothing." She wanted revenge from Chandar for her own unhappiness.

"You witch, you're going too far, now that you have everything that belongs to Bhaiya. Masi was right, if you stumble into a gutter your entire body will be covered in filth. You're getting married, I don't care what happens to you anymore." Chandar turned to leave.

"Here are my blessings," he stopped suddenly and gave her such a resounding slap that the half-dead Chandni fell against the wall.

"Hai, you fickle man!" Usha's heart was not made of stone after all. Barre Sarkar who had been in a state of semiconsciousness suddenly got up from his chair, but Usha restrained him.

"Let him be, Didi, I'm glad he hit me. Now he will cry when he remembers me and will be filled with regret and sorrow." Chandni began to sob.

"I remember you, you worthless creature? I won't even spit on you."

"Don't say things you'll regret later, Chandarji, things that will make you hold your head and mourn." Usha was overcome by remorse. "If she does something reckless because she is upset, her blood will be on your hands." Usha found a way to shift her own wrongdoing onto Chandar's shoulders. In the morning when Chandni's dead body was discovered everyone would think she had killed herself because she had fought with Chandar.

"It's you who were born to hold your head and mourn, Usha Rani. I don't want to call you sister and insult this sacred relationship. You're not a woman, you're the crushed corpse of society's customs. You've been told only that serving your husband is your religion, but he is not even your husband! You've just been thinking of him as a husband since you were a little girl."

"Chandar!"

"You are the true daughter of Bharat, you will sacrifice your life for the person you think of as your husband, you will keep worshipping at his feet whether he cuts you up and feeds you to the dogs. You're not a woman, you're a bondmaid." He turned to go.

"Wait!" He was conditioned to being startled by Barre Sarkar's voice. He stopped reflexively.

"Ask Kiran to forgive you," he said sharply.

"Kiran?"

"Yes, this is not Chandni, her name is Surya Kiran from now on."

"Ahhhaha—this is great!"

"Don't be rude, or else…"

"Or else what?"

"You will have to leave this house."

"Do you think I have any desire to live here now? But don't think for a minute that I'm leaving because I'm afraid of anyone. No. It's because this house is driving me mad."

"Kiran, forgive Chandar, he's very foolish."

"Chandar is very foolish, you're very wise."

"Chandni, go to your room, you should rest," Usha said.

"Yes…Usha Didi is also very wise, she knows what has to be done, what time one should wake up, when one should sleep, who should live and who should die," she muttered as she turned to leave.

Barre Sarkar looked greedily at the dazed Chandni. Her dupatta had slipped from her shoulders, a sudden breeze made her clothes cling to her body. He lunged towards her.

"No...!" Her old fear returned. Hearing Usha's muffled sob she felt like clawing his face. Why was Usha so crazy about this wretched animal? "Make preparations for the wedding, everything should be ready, should be perfect," she said and left.

When she returned to her room she heard Chandar and Pimo talking in the corridor outside her room.

"Chot Bhaiya, listen," Pimo was running after him.

Pimo would also hate her now. Chandni went to the window and looked at the rocky peaks in the distance. Pimo came into the room quietly and stared silently at her. Pimo was her friend, her confidante, but she adored Chandar.

She couldn't say anything. Quietly she began packing her suitcase.

For a split second Chandni was overcome by the desire to put her arms around Pimo and tell her everything, because when she died who would explain the real reason behind her death to Chandar and Pimo? And Chandar wouldn't worship her, he would forget her. She wouldn't even be able to hold on to that in the valley of death.

She glanced at the vial in her hand, then put it into her purse. No, she couldn't die just yet. For a long time she kept writing on a piece of paper and kept erasing what she had written with her tears.

"Chandar, everything will be all right, when the time comes you'll understand everything," Usha said, putting away his clothes in his suitcase.

"There's nothing left in life that can be all right."

"Very soon you and Pimo will be back."

"I won't come back even when I'm dead."

"Is it possible for brothers to be separated forever? You don't know how ill he is right now. What I say is..."

"I've never understood what you say and never will. You're not a human being, you're a stone. He treats you so badly and you continue to worship him, and today you really went too far. You're handing him over happily to another woman."

"I've not handed him over to anyone, and as long as I'm alive no one can take him from me. I brought him back from the jaws of death, but how can I tell you…one day all will be revealed…the family's welfare is paramount. Here, take this cheque, Chachaji will have it cashed for you. I'll see that the car is brought around. And listen, make sure Pimo doesn't feel too disheartened. If she sees you getting so upset she'll curl up in a corner and cry."

"Didi, I'm terrible, I've been saying such terrible things to you, can you forgive me?" Chandar grabbed her feet.

"Arre, what are you doing, my brother! Are you crazy? How can I be offended by anything you say?"

"Maa left us when we were children, you were the one to give us all the comfort a mother gives her children. I had thought that one day you and Bhaiya…Didi, my blood boils to think…but I'm helpless, what can I do? What will you do here now?"

"This is my house," Didi smiled.

"Listen Didi, you won't be happy here, come with us, we'll all live happily somewhere else."

"Now only my funeral bier will leave this house. My dear brother, trust me, but listen, if you hear some bad news don't lose heart."

"What kind of news, Didi?" Chandar looked worried.

"News of the wedding," Usha laughed.

"Arre, I'm repelled by the very sight of her face."

"No, Chandar…" she stopped in mid-sentence.

"What?"

"Nothing. I will send your breakfast."

Finally Usha hugged Pimo, instructed her to take care of Chandar and said goodbye to them.

"Pimo…Pimo…" Chandni ran after them as the car left the house. It stopped, Chandni leaned in through the window hesitantly and placed her hand on Pimo's cheek. Pimo's tears streamed down her face and she quickly turned away. Chandar asked the chauffeur to start the car.

"Pimo, Pimo, look at me once…you won't see me again, Pimo…" She began running alongside the car, stumbled and fell on the gravelly road. The string of wax beads that Chandar had given her on her birthday instead of the necklace broke, and the beads scattered everywhere. She stared wildly at them. All at once they dissolved and became pearls. Her head dropped.

Silence reigned over the haveli, as if a death had taken place. Chandni stayed quietly in her room. She was no longer afraid of anyone. Seeing Pimo's things spread all around her heart sank, going into Chandar's room made her feel depressed—the past rushed at her.

No, she was not going to die so easily. She was alive only because she wanted Barre Sarkar's real self revealed to all. In addition, there was still a tiny ray of hope that glimmered. Maybe Chandar would believe her when he read the letter she had slipped into his pocket, and then she would gladly breathe her last in his lap.

When Usha reminded her of her promise, she lost her temper. "Didi, I've never played the dying game before. Don't remind me again and again, let me die on my own. But if you want, you can strangle me yourself or pour the poison down my throat."

When she saw Usha looking worried she broke into a laugh. "You don't want my blood on your hands because they've been made to be decorated with henna. After I die and everyone has forgotten me, you will marry Barre Sarkar. But don't worry, I am destined to die."

And Usha Rani remained silent in order to appease her, but would sing the glories of sacrifice, of giving up one's life, sang melancholy bhajans so that there were times when Chandni felt like ending her life without waiting for Chandar. But then somewhere far away she would hear the whistle of a train and hope that Chandar was on it, that everything was going to be all right.

How many friends did Barre Sarkar have? Those who were his age were now planning their children's weddings. Who knew that he would get married at this age and that also to an unknown young girl? He was quite overwhelmed by the wedding arrangements. Usha Rani was in charge of everything. As the wedding day approached, she started getting very worried. What if Chandni went back on her word? If she turned her out of the house where would she go? Whom would she turn to for support?

The fire that had been burning in her heart had abated. Romance had turned into a simple question of food and shelter. Masi, while she was alive, had been such a great support. Always instructing her to turn to Bhagwan for succour, she had trained her in such a way that she had learnt to restrain her desires. But the need to survive and her self-respect were still alive.

Wedding celebrations began and there was no sign of Chandar. Usha responded to all of Chandni's appeals with silence. Chandni felt her hopes falling into slumber in the lap of death.

The fire at the mandap was being stoked. Chandni was decked out in all Maa's jewellery. Usha went up to her on the pretext of fixing her sari's pallu.

"The time for the lagan is approaching," she said tearfully.

"I know, Didi, don't worry."

"I have to worry."

Chandni saw Barre Sarkar dressed as a bridegroom and fell into a chair with a deep sigh. The time for the last train had passed. No one came and no one was going to come!

Usha poured a glass of sherbet from the jug. Chandni took the vial from her purse and emptied its contents into the glass.

"Are you satisfied now?"

Usha lowered her eyes.

"You will tell Chandar and Pimo everything, won't you?"

"Ye…Yes…" she promised. "Come, hurry up now."

"Why the rush? The ceremony won't begin for a while," Barre Sarkar said, pulling up a chair to sit on.

Colour draining from her face, Usha stood up with a stricken look.

"Is everything all right? What's happened?"

"Nothing." She turned to leave.

"You look very nervous," he said with a smile.

"No, no, not at all. The guests are arriving, I…I…" Usha stuttered.

"Yes, of course, you should go and take care of the guests. Make sure the ice cream doesn't melt, and I think we'll need more sweets."

"No, we have enough."

"You have to do all the work, Usha."

"No, no, really…"

"Why no? You've made such excellent arrangements. No one except you and Masi had the capacity to do this." He stressed each word.

"Yes…" Usha stammered.

"Everything will be all right, yes?"

"Yes…yes, it will…"

"And you won't have any complaints left?"

"No, I won't," Usha said impetuously.

"Then go and take care of the preparations." He smiled, then glowered at her.

She left hastily, bumping into people as she walked out.

After Usha had gone, Barre Sarkar sighed deeply and gazed at Chandni with the same melancholy look. She sat quietly, her eyes on the glass.

He filled a glass with sherbet, then put it down and cautiously placed both his hands on Chandni's hands. As if stung by a snake Chandni pulled away quickly, then covering her face, broke into sobs.

"Arre, still so bashful? Wah!" He smiled wickedly. "You're happy today, aren't you?"

She gathered up all the hate in the world in her eyes and scrutinised him from head to toe. "Yes, I'm very happy." Then she picked up the glass in front of her and put it to her mouth.

"Arre, don't drink so quickly, it will go down the wrong way," he laughed, then picked up his own glass. "What's the rush?" he asked, taking a sip.

Intoxicated with a sense of victory, she pushed away his hand and, closing her eyes, began to gulp down the sherbet.

Usha Rani was with the guests but her mind was elsewhere. She wanted to be happy, but she was trembling all over.

After emptying the glass, Chandni broke into loud laughter and kept laughing, forgetting even to wipe the tears streaming down her face.

"Yes, Barre Sarkar, I'm yours now." She spread out both hands towards him.

But he fixed his eyes on her, kept smiling and continued drinking from his glass.

Suddenly Chandni clutched her throat with both hands. Standing in front of her was Chandar, looking dishevelled and worried.

Chandarji! When she realised that her eyes were not deceiving her and that Chandar was actually there, she stumbled across the room and clung to him.

"You're late, Chandarji, I'm leaving, Raja, I've drunk the poison, look there's your Surya god."

"You've come, Chandar." Barre Sarkar's voice resounded with the ring of victory and he drained his glass in one gulp.

Chandar was late. He would have been here six days earlier but he and Pimo had gone hunting with Mamaji, and it was only when they returned and his coat was being sent to the laundry that the note was discovered.

"But who can fight the fates, Chandarji?" Chandni said, touching his face with trembling hands. "Hide me inside your bosom, Chandarji, my heart is sinking." She became unsteady in his arms.

Chandar quickly put her down on the sofa. Pimo placed her face upon hers and began weeping. There was a commotion among the guests.

"Munshiji, please call the doctor, quickly." Chandar wiped the sweat from her forehead with his lips. "Please hurry."

"It's all right, Munshiji, we don't need a doctor." A twisted smile danced on Barre Sarkar's face, he was sipping the sherbet with relish, seated calmly in his chair, as if Chandni were an insect and not a human being.

"You wretch, you coward, you've taken the life of an innocent girl and you're sitting here, laughing like the devil!" Chandar leapt and grabbed Barre Sarkar by the throat and shook him violently. "But how will you escape me?"

Sarkar pushed Chandar away roughly, his face suffused with extreme anger. The Chandar who had always feared this look cowered before him for a moment.

"What kind of silly talk is this?" Barre Sarkar said gently. "Have you ever heard that a bee strangled a blossom, or a moth extinguished a flame?" He walked up to Chandni, the picture of dignity, and gently stroked her tousled hair.

"The silly girl—she thinks she has drunk the poison…"

A heartrending scream issued from Usha's mouth and she ran to snatch the glass from him, but he drained it in one last swallow.

Usha stared at him wildly, then fell down and clutched his feet.

Chandar pressed his temples, failing to comprehend what was happening.

Chandni moaned and opened her eyes. When Barre Sarkar placed a hand on the sofa to steady himself, she shrank and clung to Chandar.

"Yes, Chandar, save her. The moonlight fades away in the presence of the sun. Usha, get up, your tears are making the poison even more bitter." He tried to lift her up. "Forgive me, Usha Rani. I did not value your love, I have hurt you badly—and for that I'm being punished today. You wasted your entire life for me."

"My lord, serving you is my life." Usha placed her head at his feet. "Why did you do this?"

"I know that whatever I have done was not right. I loved Chandni. If I had loved Bhagwan as much I would have found him by now, but Chandni and Suraj cannot be one." He became dizzy and was about to fall. Chandar rushed forward and caught him in his arms.

"Bhaiya! Arre, Munshiji, have you called the doctor?"

"The doctor can't do anything now, Chandar."

"But Bhaiya, why did you have to do this?"

"There was no other way, Chandar. Usha, don't make me a greater sinner than I am by touching my feet. In trying to transform an ordinary human being into a god you turned him into the devil. Tiny lies grew into terrifying sins and…and…" He winced in pain and vomited blood.

The doctor ripped through the crowd of people to get to him, but he stopped him.

"Doctor, these last few moments of life are the most precious I have left, don't snatch them from me. You won't be able to save me. Even Bhagwan cannot avert death now." Then, driven by pain, his eyes turned inward, the bridge of his nose shifted, and in a few seconds his breath became laboured. He gazed at Chandni standing in the distance. As death approached, his eyes danced for the last time, and with a blood-soaked smile he said playfully, "Look at the silly girl, she's crying! But why are you shedding tears from afar? Come here, Chandni! Place your hand lovingly on my bosom just once…or else this heart will remain tormented for all eternity."

Chandni felt her heart sinking and she fell on his chest.

Barre Sarkar took her in his embrace, and for the first time Chandni did not resist.

"Ah, if death is so beautiful then why should one not want to be born and die a thousand times," he said, intoxicated with death and love, and placed his lifeless lips upon her forehead.

Chandni was filled with anguish. If only his chest would burst open and she could drown forever in its unfathomable depths.

"Don't cry, my love! It's your wedding today. Look, the sun is setting, today the moon will hold sway and there will be radiant moonlight everywhere."

In the west the last ray of sunshine sobbed and was silenced, and the soft, shy light of the moon spread like the shroud of a newly-wed bride.

Wild Pigeons
(*Jungli Kabutar*)

Cradling her head tightly with her hands, Abida sat motionless in the half darkness of her room. The night was slowly filling it like black smoke, but more than the atmosphere it was the deep sadness that was stifling her desolate heart. Dry-eyed, she felt as if there were sand rankling between her eyelids. In the bungalow next door the phone shrilled continuously. Perhaps the owners had gone out. From the servants' quarters came the muted sound of their conversation and the tinkling of pots and pans.

She reached out with her hand and straightened the crease in the bedcover. If only there was enough power in one's hands to smooth layer after layer of wrinkles in one's heart. Drained by a sense of anguish she turned on the lamp. One half of the bed lit up, the black and green blossoms on the bedcover came to life…part of the bed awakened but the portion where Majid had slept remained engulfed in tomblike darkness. The lamp on his side of the bed was beyond her reach but she also knew that its light would not pierce the darkness that had swallowed him.

Six months had passed since the period of *iddat*. Amma had said innumerable times, "Child, how long will you continue to ruin your life living in this desolate house?"

But Abida had turned her grief into her life. She didn't have anything else to remember him by, did she? She felt an otherness in that grief. She knew his side of the bed would never come to life, that the sudden touch of her hand could not make his body start and offer her the invitation of an embrace. The special fragrance of his cigarettes would never permeate the room, no one would potter around noisily early in the morning in the bathroom and hum songs that were out of tune, no one's bristly cheek would ever scratch her chin again.

Right next to the window the birds on the tangled vines of the Chameli were creating a real racket. A bullock-cart was creaking its way down the road. Abida got up and tiptoed her way to the almirah, opened it, and taking out one of Majid's shirts, crumpled it in her hands, carefully threw it down on the floor, then carelessly draped his pants and tie on the chair. After this she took out a cigarette and lighter from the drawer, lit the cigarette, turned on the lamp on Majid's side of the bed, and placed the lighted cigarette on the lip of the ashtray.

The desolation in the room was dispelled instantly. Abida sat down calmly on the rocking-chair and began knitting Majid's sweater.

~

Among the wedding guests at Makkan Baji's wedding she had spotted Majid Bhai laughing loudly. He was a distant cousin from her mother's side. She had never seen him before but had heard a great deal about him. He is a flirt, he has had several successful and unsuccessful romantic liaisons. Every year it was reported that Majid Bhai had married some actress. Then one would hear that yes, he was getting married, but to a friend's divorced wife. Once it was rumored that he had become enamoured of a lady doctor and a civil marriage was about to take place; the schoolteacher with whom he had had an ardent relationship was threatening to commit suicide. A lot of glamour attached to Majid Bhai's name because of all this talk. Young women loved to have long discussions about his amorous adventures.

After Bajia's wedding Abida got a chance to see Majid Bhai at close quarters. He was not at all the epitome of the young Prophet Yusuf, but when you met him you realised that there was indeed something that made for a special excitement, something that tickled your heart.

"Oh, so you are Abida," he said pointedly, the moment he met her.

"Yes. Has someone complained to you about me?" Abida retorted.

"Uhh…no, no one has complained. Did I say that?"

"The way you asked me made me think that perhaps you had."

"Well, you're very perceptive."

"Yes, thank you!" And with that she turned on her heels and walked away to help Khala Jaan in the drawing room. She was angry because her heart was beating wildly.

"My dear, could you sprinkle some pistachio slivers on the kheer in the bowls? I can't imagine what embellishments the girls are busy with," Khal Jaan said, arranging onion rings on a dish of seekh kababs.

Abida saw five or six girls engrossed in decorating the kheer by writing Bajia and her bridegroom's name on it with bits of pistachio. She looked down to see what they were writing and at that moment Shabana slapped a piece of silver paper on her lips. Shabana was Majid's younger sister and she teased every young woman by calling her "bhabi".

When Abida walked past Majid Bhai while the food was being served he quipped, "People are disposing of the delicacies under the pretext of serving others."

"Oh, so now you have knowledge of the unknown, or is there an x-ray machine in your specs which enables you to see what's inside people's stomachs," she snapped.

"No need for an x-ray of the stomach. Mouths are speaking their guilt."

That was when Shabana broke into giggles. Even after Abida had rubbed her lips vigorously, a trace of silver paper remained.

But when her gaze fell on the bowl of kheer in front of Majid Bhai she thought she was going to die. Someone had written "Abida/Majid" on it with pistachio flakes.

She thought she would switch bowls but when she extended her hand towards it, Majid Bhai stopped her. "This is mine."

"I…I…well, I'll get you another one," quickly spreading her fingers to cover the kheer.

"Why? Leave my bowl alone." Majid's fingers covered hers. Abida quickly drew her hand away.

"Oh!" Majid Bhai coloured when he discovered the secret of the bowl. Abida felt the blood draining from her body. She hastily began pouring water in the glasses.

Later she would laugh about this incident, but that day she let Shabana have it until the girl's face was swollen from weeping. And she also put Majid Bhai through the wringer, something he would never forget because Shabana, the wretch, reported everything to him.

"What did you gain by making Shabana weep like this? There were other ways of showing your dislike of me, although there was really no need to make such a production of it. I'm not an idiot." He took the opportunity to say this at another party.

"I...that is...actually, I was angry and..."

He was upset that she had been so angry with Shabana. "She's young, she thinks that all girls are as crazy about her brother as she is. She likes you, she likes you very much. As far as she was concerned she had made a very affectionate joke. She didn't have the slightest idea that she had done something you would find extremely offensive."

"I...I'm sorry. I don't know why I felt my tongue burning and I scolded the poor thing so badly." Abida wanted to disappear. What was happening?

"Listen," Majid stopped her just as she was turning to go and said, "do you believe everything anyone tells you about somebody without first checking and asking?"

"Of course not."

"Then why did you insult her?"

"I...I don't know what happened to me at that moment...I'll ask her to forgive me."

"And think about asking me to forgive you, too. If someone had said something as objectionable about you I would never have believed it for a second."

"Why wouldn't you believe it? How do you know that..."

"I know."

"What do you know?"

"I know you...my sisters give me all kinds of information about you in their letters, including details like what you were wearing on a certain day."

"Oh!" Abida began feeling angry again, but this time with herself.

"All right, so tell me what other flaws I have besides being a vagabond, and a base and dishonourable fellow?"

"None," she said lamely.

Majid Bhai turned away and began talking to some other people. And then he left. He didn't come to say goodbye. He went in to say his salaams to Ammi, while she stayed hidden inside. He never asked about her.

But within a week his proposal arrived. Bajia told Abida that he wanted to know if she was agreeable to the match and that Ammi had already said yes. "So this is just a formality."

"And what if I refuse…?"

"Ai hai, are you crazy? He's such a nice young man."

"I don't care. What if I don't like him?"

"Oh, come on, don't pretend. You're speaking nonsense, go and take a look at yourself in the mirror."

And feeling helpless, Abida burst into tears.

"Ai hai, what's wrong with him? You've given him your heart, not your honour."

"Bajia…I'm scared."

"But why?"

"I don't know."

"All right, that's enough, now don't be a fool. And in any case you're not getting married tomorrow. Majid Mian has asked permission to first correspond with you."

"No, no, and anyway, what difference can writing letters make?"

"Do you want a courtship then? My dear, you're so lucky you're getting a chance to correspond. I just saw a glimpse of your dulha bhai from a crack in the door of the cowshed. And by God, just that one glimpse made me break out in a sweat. All night, all day, it felt as though he was here, sitting in front of me and staring, teasing me with his eyes. Oh God!" Bajia rocked with laughter.

~

"I'm attracted to pretty women but no one has stolen my heart yet," Majid wrote, "and I can't promise that after marrying you I will become a dull and pious man. You are the one who will have to decide whether to take your gift back and then allow it to be given to someone else."

Abida wrote, "I don't regard the heart as something that one gives or takes. Whatever the heart is, it will always be yours. If you wish you can distribute it here and there, but remember that I can't become a person who shares with anyone else."

"You argue so stubbornly, you know. This means we can't be married," Majid wrote.

"No, that's not what it means," Abida wrote back after thinking long and hard.

~

After the wedding Abida realised how subjugated you feel when the person who has won by writing letters actually appears before you in person. Not only had she never been in love, she had never even entertained the thought of a man in her heart. She saw God's light in Majid's love. She gathered her world with both hands and let it drown in his being. But she didn't abandon her feminine pride. If Majid was ever late coming home, she would roam restlessly, staring tearfully at the door. But the moment he entered she would still the beating of her heart, appear casual and busy herself with some silly chore. When he pulled her passionately into his embrace she would restrain herself and sprinkle cold water on his ardour.

"Arre…arre…look at the carpet, is it alright?" And Majid would stop to look at the carpet, his passion cooled. She would involve him in some very dry economic or political issue just to give him as few opportunities as possible to be amorous.

And that was not all. She didn't even take off her armour on the double-bed.

Because she was afraid of him.

He was false, wasn't he?

She would often think that she had relinquished her entire existence into his hands and if he betrayed her, what would she be left with? She wouldn't want to live. And so she kept reminding him

that there were other more important things in life than him that
were of interest to her.

~

But one incident shattered her strategy. What she was afraid of finally
happened. She wanted to forget Majid's past but it pushed ahead and
grabbed her by the throat.

One day a stranger called and asked that she send Majid to the
hospital immediately. His wife had delivered a baby in Room 6. The
baby was fine but the mother was dying. J. J. Hospital.

Majid entered the house and became extremely agitated when he
saw Abida. She was still sitting next to the phone. The colour of her
henna still shone on her nails, but her body was cold and her face was
ashen.

"Your wife has had a baby," she said with a smile.

"Arre, but it's only been two months since we got married. That's
great." He heard her speak, was filled with relief and swept her into
his arms.

"Don't joke. Are you a man or a beast?" She pushed him away. "A
helpless woman has been a victim of your dastardliness and you…"

"Abida, what are you saying?"

"I called you everywhere…"

"But…"

"In J. J. Hospital…the baby is healthy, but the mother is dying."
She became hysterical.

"What is wrong with you? I swear I don't have any other wife
except you."

"So, did you divorce her? You beast…the mother of your child!" If
she could have had her way she would have strangled him with her
bare hands. Majid tried to calm her but she scratched his face, tore
his clothes and then, burying her face in her hands, began sobbing
bitterly.

"Abida, for God's sake, please listen to me."

"Don't touch me! You think I'm crying because I'm feeling let down by my fate, but that's not it. By God, I'm crying for that unfortunate woman whom you have betrayed."

"Oh God, what is all this?" Majid collected his thoughts and called J. J. Hospital.

"Can you please tell me the name of the patient in Room 6?"

After several inquiries it became clear that Room 6 was empty.

"Ohhhh…so the poor woman has died…Oh my God, you're a murderer…you killed her…and your son…what will happen to that unfortunate child…he will be raised in an orphanage…no…he won't be raised in an orphanage…he didn't get a mother's love and his father is a devil."

The situation became unmanageable. With great difficulty witnesses were produced to swear that no one had delivered a baby in Room 6 and no woman had died there. A patient, Lalaji, suffering from indigestion had been admitted to the hospital and he too had left two days earlier. Then finally the riddle was solved. Majid's friend who was responsible for this tasteless joke had thought Abida would be greatly amused by his prank. Several arguments later it was agreed that this was the stupid friend's fault, and Abida's own way of thinking had contributed to her state of mind. The story faded away, but Abida couldn't forget what had happened to her after the phone call. Again and again she was tormented by a nightmare in which she had had a baby in the hospital, she was dying, and Majid's new wife was looking everywhere for him. And Abida finally breathed her last in Room 6.

But ten years passed and the dream was not realised. The doctors finally gave up. Both are healthy. There's no reason not to conceive.

~

"Please come back, for God's sake." Majid's latest letter lay before her. Telegrams and letters were pouring in. "Ammi Jaan is not well," she would reply. Majid's mother had suffered a second attack of paralysis. He and Abida had come to see her and Abida had stayed back to nurse her. Now the old lady neither died nor recovered. "How can I leave her alone? Why are you in such a state? Find someone to fall in love with for the time being, it will help you pass the time." She wrote all this just to tease him and Majid would get riled up in response.

"Why, have you forgotten all your tricks in ten years?" she tantalised him. "You poor thing."

"You're asking for it," he replied irately.

Eventually Ammi Jaan improved but then Makkan Baji arrived to deliver her sixth baby. Abida was the only one without children, everyone else was busy tending their offspring.

"Should I leave Baji alone here in this condition?" she wrote to Majid.

"No, there's no rush, but for God's sake come back immediately after this," he replied wearily.

Six months passed in all this back and forth. When she returned she found Majid looking very glum and unhappy. But Abida got busy with tidying up the house. No linen in sight, no towels, plates and dishes a mess, half the pots and pans on loan to the neighbours.

"For God's sake, just buy new pots so we can put an end to this," Majid snapped, worn-out by all this talk about pots, pans and cutlery. But Abida had only one thing on her mind. Until she got the house in shape again she could not rest.

After fixing the bedroom, drawing-room and kitchen, she turned her attention to clothes. Half of Majid's clothes had disappeared. Her own saris were not all there. Except for the simple and very expensive ones, nearly all the others were missing.

And she was worried the most about Majid. Half of him had disappeared as well. His face looked sad and he appeared somewhat lost. Busy with getting the house in order, Abida had failed to notice this at first and he had been quiet as well.

"You're back, but still far away," he protested.

"Do you see that the house has turned topsy-turvy? My tin of talcum powder has also disappeared. I don't know what to complain about any more."

"You hated the smell of the powder."

"I didn't hate it. You're the one who made a fuss about it. Anyway,

I don't care that it's gone, I want to know who cleaned out the house like this."

"I did," Majid said guiltily.

The cigarette ash fell on the tablecloth. In an instant she ran back to the room from the past. This long journey had tired her out. She placed the sweater she was knitting on the arm of the chair. When it was completed she would hang it up next to the sweater she had finished last week.

She gave herself up to grief and stretched out on her side of the bed. Tears flowed down her cheeks and wet her hair. She placed a hand gently on the pillow next to hers and turned back to the past. She had repeated each incident so many times in her mind that now she didn't need to make an effort to remember.

~

"She works at the canteen?"

"How many times will you ask?"

"As often as you say you don't love her." There was the stillness of death in her voice.

"Well, in that case this discussion will never end."

"You still think I shouldn't leave the house after this?"

"Yes."

"What will I do in this big rambling house after you've left…"

"No."

"But…"

"I can't live without you." Majid spoke like a stubborn child. Abida felt like clawing his face but she only smiled. Majid avoided her gaze.

"I'll leave by the morning train," she said determinedly. "You won't be able to leave by the morning train, it won't be possible to make arrangements for the funeral that early in the morning."

"The same threats again! Just think about what you're saying. I'm not made of steel."

"That's what I thought. I wish I could break down the wall of your restraint! I wish you would scratch my face like an ordinary woman. But you're not an ordinary woman, you're Abida, I didn't even have the courage to fall at your feet and ask forgiveness for my sins."

"There's no point in making these depressing comments. It's your duty to be fair. I don't want you to betray her as well."

"Abida, the softness of your voice is paralysing me. The only reason I haven't done what I should have done till now is that I had hoped, since you are different from other women, that you would think about my mistake objectively."

"What is it that you should have done and haven't done till now?"

"I have no right to live. If a man who is deficient cannot be forgiven then there's only one recourse left."

"In other words, suicide."

"Absolutely."

"Why do you entangle me in these romantic notions?" Adida said wearily.

"Abida, if I've picked up an ember by mistake should I hold it in my palm and fan it forever?"

"This is a ridiculous example. You've always played with fire. For ten years you lived an unfamiliar and unnatural existence, and the minute you got a chance you returned to your true self." Abida's tone hardened. Majid felt encouraged.

"Abida, if you had committed such an error I would never have punished you like this. Do you really think that I can spend my life with this empty-headed, illiterate woman?"

"If she was really so uninteresting how did she become your precious beloved?"

"But if one enters a toilet to urinate should one be incarcerated there? Can one spend one's entire life in such a place? I never claimed that I was an angel. You know perfectly well that I'm a weak, deficient human being, but I don't deserve such harsh punishment. Just think, if I could tolerate her what was there to stop me? I wouldn't have needed your insistence, I would have left you without a qualm. Would you have stopped me?"

"Absolutely not."

"You are definitely pushing me away with both hands. If I had the slightest bit of self-respect I would have left immediately."

"What if I had made a similar mistake?"

"By God, I would have smashed your bones, but I wouldn't have punished you for living with a wild beast."

"What do you want?"

"I want you to punish me as you see fit. If you're revolted by me, I promise I won't touch you without your permission. We can live like two friends, can't we?"

"But why must friends live with each other? She needs you, how will she battle life alone?"

"You're feeling very sorry for her."

"She's pitiful. And what will become of that innocent child? You will have to marry her."

"Abida…" Majid got up and started pacing restlessly. "I am… whatever you decide, I am ready to do, except marry her. Don't give me this cliched, worn-out punishment, I won't be able to endure it. You don't get married because of some compulsion or pressure."

"But an innocent—"

"I'm not refusing monetary assistance, and there will be all the publicity to deal with as well."

"Monetary assistance? I didn't know you regarded money as being so important. Will monetary assistance atone for everything?"

"I hate the idea of saving face. To get married just to protect one's image would be a betrayal of my conscience. I cannot embark on a long journey with this girl."

"Don't be so dramatic, I understand only too well. But if you weren't so concerned about her, why did you give her my saris?"

"Only because I hated them and so I threw them away," Majid said listlessly. "Abida, have I committed a sin that has never been committed before? Has no one ever been guilty of such stupidity? I've explained to you several times, I was troubled. I wrote you numerous letters, sent you telegrams, you didn't come. I wrote in clear terms that I needed you. Pick up my letters and read them. I even said that my life and my convictions are being threatened, for God's sake save me."

"How could I leave Ammi Jaan, and then there was Baji's pregnancy."

"So if I had died you would still not have returned? Compared to my mother and sister, I am nothing?"

"God forbid, if you were ill…"

"You mean to say I wasn't ill?"

"This is not an illness."

"My love, this is the world's most horrible illness. It has caused the greatest of saints to become weaklings."

"Uff, you're just trying to make a case for what you did."

"Abida, I don't at all expect you to forgive me and clasp me to your breast, although by God I'm ready to give up three-fourths of my life for such a miracle. I know I cannot regain the place I once had in your heart, which I have now lost. But I do beseech you, please meet her once and then decide. If you still want to stick with your decision after that, you will get what you want."

"I know I can never win with you. I will have to change my principles. You can marry a second time, you have my permission."

"Marriage is a sacred vow, it can't be made with anyone who happens to come your way, nor can it be undertaken again and again."

"You can fall in love with anyone who comes your way?"

"If someone falls into the gutter it doesn't mean they have fallen in love with filth. If the union of bodies doesn't involve the soul, you can't call it love. There's a difference between love and lust."

"Oh my God!" She clasped her head between her hands. She was surprised by how casually she was talking about the most horrible accident of her life. Her heart was devoid of all emotion.

"I won't beg for my life any more." What would she have done if he had come down to using force like other men? "I've said this before, the girl has no substance."

"But her body is not without substance," Abida taunted.

"Her body, too…has brought so much anguish for me that I'm now revolted by it. Abida, I thought a hundred times that I should get rid of her before you come back. How will I look you in the eye? But without hearing the verdict from your own mouth I couldn't even die."

"Oh dear, the same juvenile threats. Do you ever think of Ammi Jaan's advanced age? Let her die peacefully first. To inflict the grief of an only son's death on her would be the worst kind of cowardice."

"There's no room to move, no way to go forward."

"If you're thinking of the child…give her a divorce after the nikah."

"If a deficient man like me is forced to become a father, what pride will the child have in me? He will become an orphan before he is born. This marriage and divorce game is not something I can manage."

On this double-bed hearts had throbbed with a love and passion that became life's single purpose. Here they read books together all night and made love, then talked and made love again and chatted again—they never tired of each other, never once felt the ache of childlessness.

On that same bed now, two strangers sat together till it was morning.

A hazy light hung about the room. The sound of a child's whimpering carried over from the cook's chamber. Husband and wife's wretched faces were as pale and lifeless as dust. This was not the wakefulness of the wedding night, it was that night of eternal despair, dark even in the light of the sun. There were blue circles under Majid's eyes. The ashtray was heaped with cigarette stubs. Both were exhausted and had squeezed themselves into their respective spaces on the bed.

On Majid's forehead sparkled burnt silver strands. Abida wanted to forget everything and place her parched lips on his unshaven chin and let the tears that had been dammed for many lifetimes flow unchecked.

Then this horrible nightmare will end and she will wake up.

~

Making every effort to protect her sandals from the sludge in the gutter, she drew her sari pallu in front of her nose and kept going. At the doorstep of a house an old woman suffering from acute asthma was blowing her breath through the pipe in her bosom, in the hotel the radio was blaring away, naked children sat astride the gutter, a kitten was seriously attacking a scrap of paper. The news of her arrival was spreading. People were leaning over their balconies to look down at her.

Mona opened the door, gazed at her through half-shut eyes and then, leaving the door open, walked back in. This was meant to indicate permission to enter. Sitting on a high uncomfortable chair, Abida thought, why did I make the mistake of coming here? Why didn't I believe what Majid had said?

Mona was an attractive girl with a filled-out body. At this moment it was more filled out than it should be and she was also walking stiffly, as if wanting to remind Abida that, "the blessing for which you have been consulting doctors for ten years has been forced on me. I have to endure your torment."

"Do you…want him to marry you?" Abida's mouth was dry, something seemed to be moving with a loud thump at the back of her throat, and her temples throbbed. She shouldn't have come into the war zone after a whole night of wakefulness and emotional turbulence.

"Is there a medal for marriage that you received and that I will get, too?" She lit a cigarette, drew on it, then blew the smoke out slowly through her mouth and nose. Abida liked the fragrance of men's cigarettes, but this one was stifling her.

"What do you want then?"

"I want to find a cure for this nuisance." She threw the cigarette on the floor, stubbed it with her foot, clapped her hand to her mouth and made a dash for the bathroom.

The sound of her vomiting shook Abida to the core. What if it reached Ammi Jaan's ears? Once, because of indigestion, she had vomited early in the morning and seeing her, Ammi Jaan had been led to believe that distributing sweets was in order. Mona returned from the bathroom, wiping her eyes, and fell wearily into her chair. There was silence for a time.

"If you want to get rid of this nuisance, rest assured arrangements can be made." Majid's child! The entire family's most wanted child! She would raise it herself.

"And you will take care of the business in the meantime?" Mona said with a smirk. Abida held back her anger and frustration. This holding back was becoming second nature to her.

"Yes," she said good-naturedly. "You're concerned with money, you'll receive your payments every month."

For a while Mona looked at Abida pityingly. "You're barren?" she asked quietly. "How fortunate you are."

"One's fortune is not in one's hands."

"Don't you hate your husband?"

"No."

"And what about me?"

"What will hating you get me?"

"Damn what you get or don't get, but if you had snatched my husband I would have killed you."

Abida wanted to tell her she would never do that, but she ignored her impulse. Why engage with someone who is bent on being belligerent?

"But you really are an angel," said Mona softly. "I lose my temper easily these days. People in this neighbourhood are very mean. My landlady is a vile woman. If I miss even a month's rent she will throw me out on the street. I've lost my job because of your darling husband. They were teaching me typing and shorthand. I didn't know he was so inexperienced that he would get me into trouble like this."

"If you like, I can find you a place to live. I have a friend in Poona." Abida changed the subject.

"Your friend? She'll let me stay with her?"

"Of course she will. We don't have to give her all the details. Anyway, she's in England these days. She won't be back for a year."

"I'll die if I live there alone."

"I'll live with you."

"You?"

"We'll hire a servant. I'll tell him you're my sister."

"You really are an angel," she said mischievously, as if she was actually saying "You are a fool and an idiot."

~

Abida was packing and Majid was sitting in the armchair, his eyes closed. He couldn't even take her to the station because Mona would be there. She was becoming more and more bad-tempered with each passing day, not enjoying nurturing her pregnancy in this isolated place. Abida sewed tiny frocks for her and napkins. Sometimes, watching her so engrossed, Mona would flare up and blurt out her nastiness.

"It would be better if it dies."

And Abida would tremble fearfully, as if someone had cursed her own baby.

"Do you love that bastard? Aren't you furious? Why don't you leave that rascal?"

She would hold Majid responsible for all the problems she had faced before she became pregnant. "Arre, you're still young, I swear you'll find a nice husband. Have you never been in love? Slept with anyone? I mean besides that vile man!" And then she would start scratching her drum-like belly.

"We have olive oil, why don't you use it? It will reduce the itching," Abida would say kindly, and Mona would fly into a rage and begin cursing.

"Put it in yours!" Then she would burst into tears and fill the entire universe with foul language. Head lowered, Abida would continue knitting the baby's sweater.

"I will wring the neck of that wretched baby," Mona threatened. Or she would say, "I won't give you what's mine, I'll turn it into a muddle like myself. And if the wretch takes after his father he'll be hoodwinking all the women he comes across. How can you tolerate that awful man? You are a Sayyed, you won't even touch anyone's left-over food. Don't you feel repelled?" She began comparing him with snakes and scorpions. Abida felt paralysed. As if her blood had stopped at her brain. Except for Majid and a very few close friends, no one suspected anything. Mona had grown up in Lahore. After completing eighth class in Lucknow, her inclinations brought her to Bombay. She kept taking up minor jobs on one pretext or another. The unfortunate girl was quite stupid. Instead of occupying a sixty-rupee-a-night room she could have stayed at the Taj. She looked unrespectable. Wasn't interested in household chores. But she dressed well and frequented high-class hotels.

Right now, wearing Abida's dressing gown, she looked like a large ball of cotton. Abida's maternal uncle had brought her the gown from Paris. She was trying hard to cope with this wretched creature. Once she signs the papers handing the baby over, the rest can be seen to. Mona had guessed as much and kept threatening her.

Abida suffered half the labour pains. The contemptible woman cursed non-stop, calling Majid all sorts of names. When Abida tried to placate her she pushed her away with such force, that if the nurse hadn't been there to grab her she would have taken a bad fall.

She didn't send Majid a telegram about the birth of the girl because she wanted to tease him, but circumstances had shaken her to such an extent that she could no longer think. The girl had taken after her father's side of the family. Majid's blood and hers, too, was coursing in her veins. It didn't seem as if she was a stranger. Because of the family resemblance she could pass for her own daughter. And if she lived with them she would absorb some of their ways. Abida suddenly began experiencing strong maternal feelings towards her. People say that if such feelings are genuine a woman will start producing milk.

When she returned home with soup and pure ghee she was stunned to see Mona nursing the baby.

"Ohh…she bites!" Mona whimpered and then broke into a laugh.

Abida felt as if someone had plunged a knife in her heart and twisted it. In two days they would be discharged from the hospital. She tried to take the baby from Mona so that she could place her in the cradle.

"Let her be. We'll wait for the nurse," said Mona.

"Why, can't I pick up a baby?"

"Oh yes, you've had hundreds of babies, haven't you?"

Mona tone was confrontational.

"How many babies have the nurses had? They take care of them."

The nurse came in just then and the matter was shelved.

~

"What kind of name is Sabiha? Catherine, Cathy…that was my mother's name."

The name Cathy made Abida feel sick. She had decided, before she was married, that if she ever had a daughter she would name her Sabiha, and if it was a boy, well…

But when Mona flatly refused to leave the baby, saying a little thing like that couldn't survive without her, Abida said the baby would be given a bottle.

"She'll die if she gets milk from a bottle."

"Why will she die? The nurse is already giving her Ostermilk."

"That's because I'm not producing enough yet. The doctor has suggested a medicine."

"But if we have to wean her then why the pills?"

"Why should we wean her? Mother's milk is good for the child." She avoided looking directly at Abida.

Abida's heart sank.

"Why are you looking at me like that? What I'm saying is correct."

"But you…you…will you raise the child? You…"

"I'll hire an old woman, or get an ayah who won't cost too much."

"So you've decided?"

"Decided what?"

"You said you wanted to get rid of this menace."

"I wanted that once, but now she is my life…my doll…Cathy darling!"

She began drooling over the baby, then looked up angrily at Abida and said, sounding frightened, "You want to take away my daughter. I won't give her up! I'll never, never give her up. Whom can I call mine except her? You don't have to pay the hospital bill, I'll work hard and

pay the last penny. I don't want your clothes, I don't want anything."
She started sobbing loudly.

"Mona…think carefully. You're overwrought right now. Think
about this child if not about yourself. What kind of life will you be
able to give her?"

"Why should you care? Are you the world's caretaker? I know why
you're saying all this. So that your conscience won't prick you. You'll
take my daughter and make your husband feel you've done him a
favour by attaching such importance to his sin. He'll worship you for
it, the stupid fool. I'll give her up to an orphanage but I won't hand
her over to you…Yes…that's why you've been so thoughtful, making
all those clothes…you want to fill the emptiness of your womb by
taking my daughter. What woman would be so concerned otherwise
about looking after her husband's bastard offspring?"

Abida felt as if the passages in her lungs had dried up, as if the
blood was no longer flowing to her brain, and in a few minutes she
would start smouldering like dry wood. She closed her eyes and
leaned back.

Suddenly Mona realised her callousness. She jumped up and
grabbed hold of Abida's feet.

"Sorry, Didi…please forgive me…Take the wretch. I'm
despicable…you did so much for me. Please forgive me."

Abida wanted to abandon the wretch that very minute and leave,
but realised it would be better for her to suffer this indignity quietly.
She pacified Mona and helped her back to bed.

"Have you made up your mind?"

"About what?" Mona asked wearily.

"About the child."

"You're very cruel." Mona started sobbing again.

"Why are you getting so agitated? If you have to give the child
away, then it's best to sever the connection quickly so that your milk
can dry up easily. And if you're not giving it away, then there's no need
to cry, is there?"

"I don't know what to do. I feel my heart is being slashed. I'll be
able to see her, won't I?"

"Of course, whenever you want."

"How will she know who I am? She'll think of you as her mother. Will she see me as one of her own?"

"Auntie, or you…" Once again Abida felt she was being stifled.

"My daughter will call me Auntie…!" She set off again. "And she'll call you Mama, and him, what about him…she'll call him Papa, won't she?"

Abida had decided that the child would call her Amma and call Majid, Abba. She hated Mama and Papa. But she didn't think it was appropriate to engage with this packet of poison.

The days spent in the hospital were like being hung on a crucifix. Mona kept changing her mind. Sometimes she would say the girl would be nothing but the bane of her existence, then suddenly threaten to kill herself if she were separated from her. Or she would start swearing at Abida and heap curses on Majid and his family.

Abida wanted a decision to be made before they left the hospital. Her friend was returning from Europe and she didn't want everyone in the family to get to hear the story. On the last day she left for the hospital, her mind made up that the situation had to be resolved one way or another, but when she arrived there the ground slipped from beneath her feet.

Mona had left with the baby. Left behind her bangles and a locket as a guarantee in the office and gone off in a taxi. In her haste she had picked up just one set of clothes and one blanket for the baby, leaving everything else behind. Abida quietly picked up the jewellery, paid the bill and returned home.

Majid opened the door when she got back. Seeing her empty-handed he didn't understand what was going on because she was beaming with joy. He thought perhaps she had found an ayah.

Abida was talking at top speed. "Hai, she's so sweet and her mouth is so delicate, the eyes I think are gray, but the nurses said that all newborns have eyes like that, maybe they'll turn brown, because her hair is brown, soft, like silk…in the beginning the hair is always silky, after the *aqiqa* it will be thicker, she looks bald like Abba Jaan but the doctor says…" She stopped suddenly.

First Majid was smiling at her excited chatter, but when she kept on talking he began feeling a little sheepish. She was giving him details about the baby as if she were describing her niece, a blood relative. She was still smiling, actually once in a while she would break into a laughter. Majid didn't have the courage to question her about anything, he was feeling quite uneasy. Abida had brought back everything she had taken for the baby. So where was the baby?

"And pink really suits her. Light pink looks good on every baby, but bright colours like yellow and red won't suit Kitty." She was rummaging through the clothes in the suitcase.

"Kitty?" Majid gaped at her foolishly. How tired she looks, he thought.

"Yes, Catherine is a nice name... Mona's mother's name was also Catherine."

Majid was staring at the designs on the carpet. Abida was out of breath. Majid began feeling apprehensive.

"Sabiha is really a very old-fashioned name." She was trembling violently as if she had been running a great distance. "There are such nice new names now." Her words ended on a sob. "Catherine is a beautiful name, isn't it?"

"What happened?" Majid whispered.

"Arre, didn't you get my telegram? A pretty little doll has been born. You didn't get my letter either?" She seemed to be looking for something in the depths of the suitcase.

"I got it." Majid felt weighed down by a sense of guilt. "But you didn't send the adoption papers...and so..."

"I changed my mind."

"Oh."

"It's cruel to separate a baby from its mother. I'm not so selfish that I should snatch up her baby just to fill the emptiness of my womb. She doesn't need anything from me and these clothes don't suit the baby at all. She looks good in pink." Abida was beginning to feel light-headed. Majid kept looking at her in stunned silence.

She quivered like a dry leaf and fell face down on top of the suitcase.

The news about Abida's illness brought about an onslaught of relatives. Anyone who saw her pale yellow colour and felt her cold hands, sympathised. Hai, the promise born after such a long time… and lost before it could come to fruition.

Majid was shocked when Abida made no attempt to rectify this misunderstanding. If people thought she had had a miscarriage why shatter their happy delusion? Actually she was feeling as if she had indeed buried a child born of her womb.

Because of so many guests in the house husband and wife didn't get a chance to talk much. Majid was quite relieved. It would have been very strange to see the fruit of his stupidity in Abida's lap. Like a noose around his neck all the time. Mona had done him a great favour by refusing to give them the baby.

Like any ordinary husband he became rather nervous when a letter from Mona arrived at his office. There was no way he could hide it from Abida. She seemed a very loving wife in the presence of their guests, but talking to her when they were alone gave Majid the jitters. She was slowly putting the tragedy behind her and there was no point in reviving it. But when he came home he couldn't look her in the eye. Asked how she was in a serious tone, then started complaining about the heat. Then she gave him a long look and he felt as if there were needles pricking the soles of his feet.

"What did she write?" Abida asked, lovingly. For a moment he was transformed into a block of ice. How did you know, you magician? But he remained frozen.

"No, no, is everything all right?" she said quickly, when she saw him rummaging through his pockets.

Mona had asked that he beg his wife's forgiveness on her behalf and say that she was not a mother, but she had read so many books and so she must surely have some idea that she was not well-educated but that she was a mother after all. "How can she think that I will turn the baby into someone stupid like myself? I swear by Holy Mary that I will raise her to be decent and virtuous like a respectable girl. I will get a job as a typist in the factory. Please don't bring your wife into all this. She is a very noble woman. I'm afraid of her."

As Abida read the letter a smile spread over her face, and Majid felt as if he were being clobbered and insulted. He had thought that the matter would be laid to rest, that the burden his conscience had to bear would be lifted. Abida would become cheerful and chatty as she had been once. He would be granted forgiveness.

"Is it easier to send a draft or a money order?" she asked pleasantly. Majid's face fell. Is this a woman or a rock? If she clawed his face like any ordinary woman, cursed and reprimanded him, he wouldn't be sitting here like a dumb idiot. Instead of feeling grateful, he became angry. "Don't be idiotic. She's calling you names and you want to send her a money order?"

"She's doing her duty, I'm doing mine."

Majid wanted to scream, This is not your duty…it's my sin. Why are you taking it upon yourself? He took the letter from her and started shredding it.

"Arre, arre, let me take down the address." She snatched the letter from him and slipped it under her pillow.

"What will you do?"

"I'll hammer my head."

Those who had come to see Abida were busy sightseeing in Bombay. Plans were made for picnics at Elephanta, film-shoots to attend and film stars to meet; food parties were the order of the day, everyone was busy chatting and socialising, and no one was aware of the mental and physical turmoil the husband and wife were going through. Throughout this commotion and carrying their respective crucifixes, the two of them continued to smile fake smiles and pretend to be an exemplary couple. But when they lay down in their double-bed at night a stony wall rose between them.

One night, believing this wall to be an illusion, Majid tried pulling her towards him, but she was so startled that she let out a stifled scream. He turned on the lamp and saw such hatred in Abida's eyes for one fleeting moment that, stunned, he quickly drew back.

"I must have dozed off." Her smile returned the next instant and she relaxed. If Majid had wanted to he could have drawn her into an embrace, but his hands were numb.

In the days that followed, whenever he made an effort to take his wife into his arms, she would hesitate for just a few seconds and then soften, but eventually bring up Mona and Kitty, which was when Majid's last reserve of strength would give out.

"Are you still angry?" he tried to restore his old banter.

"Uff! Don't be so sentimental, it disgusts me." She too resumed her old style. "Why would I be angry?"

"You avoid me."

"Allah! Why would I avoid you? I haven't stolen anything from you, so why should I avoid you?"

"I'm the one who's done the stealing...and you're the one being punished for it."

"Don't be so melodramatic. Go to sleep now. The house is full of guests and look at you, acting silly like this."

"You just need an excuse."

"You're imagining things, that's all," Abida said in irritation.

"Tell me truthfully, how many days has it been since you kissed me?"

"All right, here..." Leaning across the rocky wall Abida placed her cold lips on his lifeless mouth. "Happy?" For a long time afterwards the two of them carried on a meaningless discussion about this delicate and fleeting touch, until their throats were dry and their eyes began to hurt. When, exhausted, they finally fell asleep they continued to sigh restlessly and kept reaching for each other.

One by one their guests were leaving. Finally, only Raffan Baji was left. Seeing Abida looking so despondent she suggested she come home with her. Abida agreed.

"Why are you going?" asked Majid resentfully.

"Baji is insistent, and I was thinking Ammi has been alone for so long."

"I'm also alone."

"You're going on a tour next month and then I'll be alone here. Farida's birthday is also approaching. I was thinking, I'll have a suit made for her with that green Chinese brocade you brought for me. I had kept it for Janee's...Kitty's birthday. Now I think..."

It sounded like she was talking to herself. Majid felt a snake had sunk its teeth in him but he didn't give up. "The house will be turned upside down again."

"This time I will put away all the good dishes and give you the keys for the few things you need every day."

"Will you also put me under lock and key?"

"You I will lock up in my heart and take you with me," she said mischievously and, pretending she hadn't seen Majid's hand coming towards her, got up quietly and started pulling out the suitcase under the bed. Like an idiot Majid pretended to be looking under the pillow for something. His fingers closed on a piece of paper. He picked it up and saw that it was Mona's receipt for the money order. His blood ran cold.

"Arre, I've been looking everywhere for this." She took the receipt from him, opened the drawer, took out a beautiful file and placed the receipt in it.

That night Majid was suddenly woken up by Abida sobbing violently in her sleep.

"Abida, Abida, what's the matter?" Majid shook her and she awoke. "What is it?" she asked with a start. Her voice betrayed no sadness.

"You were crying in your sleep. Was it a bad dream?"

"No, I wasn't dreaming."

"Then why were you crying?"

"I wasn't." She ran her fingers over her face. "Arre!" She began laughing when she felt the tears on her cheeks. "But I swear I wasn't dreaming. I haven't dreamt for ages," offering all sorts of justifications.

"You must have forgotten, some dreams are not recalled."

"But I'm telling you I wasn't dreaming. You're blaming me for no reason." She got upset.

"It's not a crime, everyone dreams."

"But if I were dreaming why would I lie about it? Is there a tax on dreams that would make me lie?" raising her voice.

"Uff-oh, but…"

"I swear by the Quran. May I be blinded if I was dreaming…" She became hysterical.

"Abida, for God's sake…I didn't mean anything by saying what I did," Majid stammered in bewilderment.

"But why did you say it? Do you think I pretend, that I'm a liar?" She began crying.

"Abida, please lower your voice…please…" He took her in his arms and tried to comfort her as if she were a child. "My love…I'm sorry…I made a mistake…your nerves are…" She was as stiff as an arrow in his arms.

"But…" she suddenly became limp.

"Shhh… I said I made a mistake, alright?" Majid tried to hold her close but it seemed they couldn't remember how to hold each other in an embrace. They, who would once be bound to each other in a minute, could no longer manage it. It was as if suddenly a profusion of elbows came in the way or some important pieces of a puzzle had been lost. When he tried to kiss her mouth, he and she both found themselves in an awkward posture. His leg became numb, he pulled a muscle in his thigh, and Abida's neck twisted at an odd angle. Embarrassed, they drew apart and started massaging their respective muscles and nerves. For a while Abida sat looking drained, twisting her hands. Majid inhaled so strongly on his cigarette that his chest felt ready to burst. Then, enclosed in their separate desolation, both quietly stared at the ceiling.

"I've stopped dreaming," she said finally and, turning on her side, stared at the blank wall.

Having come to the conclusion that once the guests had left and the house was empty Abida would go mad, Majid did not discourage her when she started packing. He felt that in her mother's home, the constant hustle and bustle of relatives coming and going would help her become normal again. Her health would also improve. Ammi Jaan was going to Nainital for the summer. There, surrounded by fun-filled activities, her anger and sadness would diminish.

"All the world's children are ours." He had never fretted about being childless. There was such a profusion of children in the family that everyone admired those who remained childless. The beautiful life that these two had shared would never have been possible had they had children. That is why people called Majid his wife's slave. The only ones who knew the secret were the couple themselves and one or two close friends who were even more cautious than them. Despite all the mental and emotional anguish and all this distancing between them, their act was intact and they were regarded as the exemplary lover and beloved.

Abida's letters reassured Majid that she was immersed in parties, engagements, weddings, celebrations for newborns, films, and picnics. She also wrote spiritedly:

"Ammi Jaan has no idea that her wish has been fulfilled. Some astrologer told her that you are not fated to have children. She wept bitterly. How my blood boiled. I wanted to claw the astrologer's face. What a thug! But what a tragedy, I say, that she is deprived of this happy news."

Then she would joke and start poking fun at their lives:

"My love, I've forgotten to put a lock on the box with the china. Well, it's foolish to lock it. Let the wretched dishes and plates break. We can get more. Don't forget to send the money order."

"Abida, Abida, my love, when will you come back…when will you bring your soul back with your body? I can't tolerate this dark chamber. I saw you in a dream last night. You were holding a bowl of kheer on which Shabana had written Abida/Majid with pistachio flakes and you were getting angry. I was laughing. You won't believe this, but when I woke up my face was covered with tears. I'm very alone. Please come back now."

"Your letter made me laugh. All this sentimental, romantic talk is boring. It seems as if you first read masnawi zehr-e-ishq and then sit down to write your letters. It hasn't even been a full month and already you are asking me to come back. And listen, before you go, give Bhai Siddiq the cheque to mail. If you don't take care of the expenses I'll keep worrying. Tani is already walking. Baji insists I adopt her and is threatening to make it legal. I laugh. All children are mine as well. A daughter is not something you trade. Just thinking about this gives me the jitters. Shabana and Manzoor are expected soon. Everyone is insisting that I take care of them. I've become an expert at taking care of deliveries. Knitting a sweater now, and the rest of the clothes are all ready. Some Baji will hand down. She writes that if it's a girl she'll call her Sabiha, and she'll leave her here

and go to England. It seems that Allah's believers are more generous than He is."

Sting, sting, sting. Majid was tired of these poisoned barbs. His bags were packed for the tour, but he wanted to go straight to Abida give her a slap and say, "You're my wife, you're my life's desire, I have rights over you, don't make me beg any more, come into my arms... come."

And she came! When he opened the door he saw her standing on the edge of the stairs, smiling. In the mysterious misty darkness of the evening, the silver dots on her cottony-white sari twinkled faintly.

She walked past him, pressing against him lightly, threw her purse on a chair and sat down on her special chair, looking serious, as if she had always sat on that chair, had never left it. Her body had filled out a bit, her complexion had bloomed and motherhood had removed the hardness from her face.

"What are you doing here?"

"What a stupid question. I felt like coming so I did." She shook her foot casually.

"Look...you..."

"Uff-oh, stammering like a virgin again."

"..." Majid picked up the purse from the chair and thrust it into her hand.

"Thanks." She slipped off her sandals, crossed her legs on the chair and, taking a mirror from her purse, began examining her half-open mouth.

"Look, Mona, if you want to make a laughing stock of us, that's a different matter..." Majid's throat was dry.

"When did I say that you had deceived me?" She was trying to hold back her laughter.

"Our friendship..."

"Friendship?" She batted her eyelashes, smiling.

"Whatever...that was...was." He corrected himself quickly. "I never promised to marry you."

"Arre, do you think I'm here to get married to you? Wah!" She burst out laughing.

"Then…you can leave."

"I can leave, but why should I?" she snapped. "Am I stealing something from you or asking you for anything? You should have asked me why I'm here." She became tearful.

"All right…so tell me why are you here?"

"I will tell you," she replied, "but why are you scolding me? Am I your wife that I should be afraid of you?"

"My wife…don't talk about her. Tell me what you want."

"You're making me nervous. Why don't you sit down?" Majid sat.

"Do you know Saran?"

"No."

"He knows you very well…no, no, by God, I haven't told him anything, he knew everything already."

Majid's face turned red. "And so?"

"So I met him in Sholapur."

"Vinod Saran, Shakuntala's husband?"

"Yes, the same."

"Your friend's…"

"So? Shakkan is my friend and that's why…he takes such good care of me."

"You came here to tell me this?"

"Yes." She lowered her head and fixed her gaze on the shiny stars on her sandals.

"That he is your friend's husband…or that he takes very good care of you, I don't know why." Majid's tone became bitter. "Yes, that's why I came, to tell you this."

"But why do you need to tell me?" said Majid, feeling stifled. "Because you also took very good care of me."

"I still take care of you…I was about to send you your cheque." He took it out from the drawer.

"Oh, thanks."

He thought she would throw it in his face, but she took it quietly and put it in her purse. Majid was disappointed.

"What was I saying? Yes, that you take very good care of me, and more than you…it's your wife who takes care of me. I have to say,

she's a remarkable woman." Suddenly her tone hardened. "A woman
of such patience…suffocates me! Anger, revulsion, these one can
cope with…but…her smile drives me mad. It would be fine if she
yelled and screamed, but the way she smiles makes me feel so low
and unclean."

"Weren't you leaving? I have to get up early in the morning,"
Majid said curtly. Mona's conversation was agitating his mind. He
didn't want to admit anything even to his own conscience.

"So, what is your opinion? Is Saran untrustworthy?"

"I don't know," Majid replied roughly.

"Unh! Maybe he's a scoundrel, but what can he do to me? He
says I shouldn't live in that filth. He has a flat on Peddar Road and
another one in Santa Cruz. I like the one in Santa Cruz. It's far from
everything else. What do you think?"

"I don't know anything." Feeling nothing but intense dislike,
Majid turned away.

"Uff-oh, what airs you put on. I know you don't want to give your
opinion, but whatever I'm doing I'm doing for Kitty."

"You receive money regularly for her expenses."

"And I have no expenses? Should I survive on air? How can a
mother, daughter and one servant manage in Bombay with your Rs.
300? If you were giving us 500 it would be different."

"Yes…but Shakuntala…your friend…"

"She is my friend and the poor girl did a lot for me when I really
needed help. Why, don't you see, if I don't accept Saran's offer he'll get
someone else?" She laughed mischievously. "And my sacrifice won't
make any difference."

"I can't offer an opinion."

"Uff! You weren't such a bore once. Tell me truly, don't you miss
me at all?"

"Our relationship was temporary and physical."

"Is there any other kind of relationship between a man and a
woman?"

"Yes, there's an intellectual relationship as well, a kind of…a kind
of meeting of minds."

"And I, unfortunate creature that I am, have no mind at all. Just this clay body." She looked at him in a strange way. "And the body has no memory, your body doesn't even remember, doesn't miss." She was slowly advancing towards him.

Majid moved to the drawer and busied himself looking for cigarettes.

"My body doesn't forget…whenever I see Kitty, it remembers." She edged towards the door as she spoke.

Majid lit a cigarette to hide the shaking of his hands.

"I don't know why you are not like the others. When I'm with you, for some reason I feel as if I'm not committing a sin, as if our relationship is sacred. You've given me a strange something that can't be found anywhere else. May the Holy Mother forgive my sins. I sit in front of her for hours and beg…Mother, bless me with peace."

"Don't place sin on the same level as worship."

"Majid." Suddenly she placed her head on his back and broke into tears. Then she put both arms around his waist and tightened her grip.

Majid broke into a sweat. He squeezed the lighted cigarette in his fist, closed his eyes and in one violent jerk, unclasped Mona's hands from his waist and pushed her towards the door.

Her face was wet with tears. Her hair had swung loose and hung to one side.

"I'm sorry," she said haughtily as she wiped her eyes and nose with the back of her hand. "Sometimes when I see you in Kitty's smile, I feel like wringing her neck." Then, seeing Majid in this agitated state, she softened.

"Forgive me, Mona… I'm an exceedingly imperfect human being…I…Abida…"

"I know," she whispered philosophically. "I'm a prostitute, and if there had been another man in your place right now I would have chewed him alive, but…in your case, I'm also an imperfect prostitute." Her sheepish laugh masked her sadness.

The door swung shut behind her…there was a kind of sadness in the light drizzle outside as well. Majid felt needles pricking his scorched palms.

"Abida, Abida…are these the rules of friendship? I'm here and you're there, playing carom with Baji's children."

Excusing himself at dinner, he retired to his room. For half the night he tossed and turned. Got up and drank some water, walked about, tried to read, but the unravelling of the brain and the call of the body could not be erased. Before his eyes there were stars twinkling on cottony-white clouds. He tried many times to loosen the hands from his waist but it seemed as if his body was being squeezed inside a steel clamp. He had changed his shirt, but the spots where her tears had fallen burned holes in his skin. The breeze was blowing in gusts, the chameli vine against the window was dancing.

To hell with the tour. He sat up with a start and lit the bedside lamp. Suddenly he turned and saw the pillow where Abida rested her head, one hand under her chin. It seemed as if she had just got up and left…he began thinking he had gone mad. Where could she go? She couldn't run away from him. She was his wife, she had destroyed his peace of mind, but she must be sleeping peacefully. Perhaps she has had a nightmare and is sobbing, but on waking will deny altogether that she had been dreaming.

I have stopped dreaming.

Can anyone stop dreaming? Dreams sustain life. Can anyone give up living? Actually her dreams have been shattered. He will mend her broken dreams. He will kiss her eyes and fill them with stars again. Then life will return. This loneliness will disappear. Once again their two names will be illuminated on silver paper.

He dressed quickly. He had left the car keys with the driver because he was going to take him to the airport, but it doesn't matter. He will take a taxi.

He forgot to take his raincoat but the downpour had diminished. He could see, in the muddied light on the road, a shining layer of tar stuck to the surface. His only companion was a wet, solitary dog.

He was soaked by the time he reached Opera House. The taxi driver looked at him suspiciously but he had got in already.

"Duncan Road." Where was this voice coming from?

He surrendered himself to some unknown power that was

crushing him from all sides like a giant cobra. He is not at all an intellectual. He's a stupid, third class, deficient creature. He will set fire to the source of this deception. He and Abida are not compatible. He will send her the divorce papers in the post first thing tomorrow. He has no right to be in this elevated position.

Unmindful of the filth and dirt, he took long strides and turned into the street. When he took out his handkerchief to wipe his face, a tiny piece of paper fluttered like a wounded bird and landed on muddy slush. He bent down and saw it was his card. His name, address, designation, telephone number. For a moment he was exasperated. Who is this idiot?

Then, like footprints slowly sinking into the mire, the realisation sank in—he was this idiot. What is such a respectable and virtuous man doing in this muck? His eyes darted back and forth, from the card to Mona's door.

Where has he come? Where was he going? Bewildered, he turned back. The night had deepened. All the poverty and nakedness of the neighbourhood collapsed over his head. It started raining again, and leaving behind the filthy, muddy, congested streets, he fled from there.

Once he was back in the civilized world he looked at his watch in the light of the street lamp. It was 2:45, he had to catch a plane at six…there was no sign anywhere of a taxi. He kept walking. Away from the filth, away from stupidity and recklessness, towards the world of perfect men. He was not ready to leave his world, his place in it, at any cost.

He finally got a taxi at Flora Fountain, and when he reached home he was so exhausted physically and mentally that he didn't have the energy to change his clothes. He stretched out on the settee to rest. His flight was not for another two-and-a-half hours.

When the alarm went off at 4:30 he felt too weak to stretch out his hand and turn it off. His head was heavy and cramps had gripped his legs. He got up with great difficulty but then collapsed immediately. He felt so sorry for himself that he began to cry.

Heat. He wanted to thrust the blanket of flames from his being but he kept sinking into white, feathery snow up to his nostrils. At the base of his neck hung a heavy bell that struck against his temples with every breath he drew. Sometimes from the right, sometimes from the left. Strung around his spine were sinuous, rustling snakes... cottony-white slush filled his eyes...the spray of stars was rankling in his eyes like the ash of diamonds.

Wrapped in the colour of dry onion peels, Abida had spread her wings over him and was crying. On the other side bottles of milk were moving in an orderly fashion and melting icy needles were coursing through his veins...Abida...Abida...he tried to call out, but his mouth had been fastened with metallic bolts that had rusted.

When he opened his eyes and saw Abida bending over him he thought it was a dream...Abida who had stopped dreaming but had assumed the form of a permanent dream herself. He was too exhausted to confront these dreams.

But when she placed a trembling hand on his forehead he was fully awake.

"You...you...how?" He tried to get up.

"Don't get up..." She was sobbing.

"Why...why are you crying?" He ran a finger down her wet cheek and closed his eyes wearily.

When he opened them again it was morning. Abida's pink gharara and dupatta were wrinkled. A lock of hair had fallen over her forehead, but tears were spilling from her eyes.

His fever had abated after ten days. What he did in those ten days, what world he inhabited, he remembered nothing. He was terrified that he had lost ten days of his life.

"What happened?"

"Rheumatic fever."

"When did you come?"

"Shankar sent me a telegram and when I came..." she was laughing and crying at the same time. "Hai, you...you scared me." Abida lifted his hand and placed it on her cheek.

"Will you leave me alone again?" Majid said, stroking her lower lip.

"When did I leave you alone? My heart was always here, with you."

"In your letters…it didn't seem that way."

"Arre, I wrote those letters just to torment you." Abida's eyes were filled with loving sweetness.

"If you scold me any more, I'll be burnt to a cinder, by God."

"Forgive me God, forgive me…" Abida tapped her ears and smacked her cheeks. "My love, I'll never make this mistake again."

Once more, the joys of the early days of their married life returned. Friends visited all day long, flowers, fruit, sweets and books arrived in such quantities that they didn't know what to do with them. There were so many letters and telegrams that Abida piled everything on trays and arranged them on the shelves next to their bed.

During his illness Majid had been transferred to the guest room. Taking care of a patient on a double-bed poses problems. When he was able to walk with some support she brought him back to their bedroom, but she changed its appearance entirely. There is little light on rainy days so she removed the heavy drapes from the windows and replaced them with pink netted curtains. Everything in the room was either white or light and dark pink so that the effect was pleasing to the eye. The white candlewick bedspread reminded one of snow-covered ground.

A dull pain in his joints persisted in Majid's body. Constant fatigue and apathy overwhelmed him. Abida tried to keep his spirits up as if he were a little boy. Her love, like a pink canopy, shaded him. Lying in this cool shade, eyes closed, Majid pondered his good fortune. He had found Abida again after a close brush with death. The nightmare had ended. Life's journey on a smooth road had begun again.

Gradually the constant stream of well-wishers ebbed, then ended. Majid had extended his leave by another two months. The doctor had instructed extreme care. Rheumatic fever affects the heart, dietary restraint was essential. Abida cooked special foods with her own hands and insisted on feeding him herself. However, excessive displays of affection in the presence of guests were now considered unnecessary and so abandoned. And she was very strict on the matter of restraint. If Majid tried to embrace her she stopped him immediately. Kept herself busy with elaborate arrangements to avoid the slightest bit of intimacy. She would change into her night-suit after he asked her to do so many times, but instead of her attractive nightdress, she began wearing long-sleeved kurtas and loose pajamas.

Majid protested loudly. "I don't like this old-fashioned stuff, it bothers me."

"Night dresses are just so showy. I gave them all to Shabana."

"Then have new ones made."

"Why?"

"Because I want you to."

"Why do you want me to?" Laughing mischievously. "I never complain. You always wear kurta-pajama and I think you look sexy."

"But you used to wear them earlier."

"That was before. I used to crawl then, even sucked on a pacifier once."

Majid felt he had nothing to say.

"And the truth is that this juvenile behaviour no longer suits us in our old age."

"So you're old now?"

"Almost old. A difference of about ten years…"

Majid's heart sank. No…Abida had not forgiven him, and she was never going to.

"Let's stop talking about clothes. Oh, I forgot to give you your orange juice." She got up quickly and left.

Yes, what difference do clothes make? If a slab of ice is draped in brocade will it become a bride? And the slab of ice on his chest kept getting heavier and heavier.

Physically he was back to normal. He had resumed going to the office, but Abida insisted on providing nursing care round the clock. She tried to do everything to make him submit to her ministrations.

"Abida." He couldn't stand it any longer and decided to confront the issue.

"Yes," she replied lovingly.

"Am I seriously ill?"

"God forbid. Why?"

"That's what I'm asking. Why then?"

Abida didn't answer. She was tracing a vague design on the bedcover with her fingers.

"Answer me."

"If there's no answer, what should I say?" she said listlessly. "Does our marriage have no meaning?"

Abida lowered her head.

"Abida, for God's sake give me an answer."

She raised her eyes slowly and turned her gaze to look for something outside the window. She was extremely pale and tired. Her eyes filled with tears.

"Abida, my love!" He tried to take her in his arms, but felt that in his arms was not his beloved wife, but steel wires that lacked flexibility, had no elasticity.

"Uff!" She had pulled a muscle and started rubbing her neck sheepishly.

"Are there thorns in my hands?"

"No...but...I..." She was evasive.

"What...? But...?" He caught her hands and pulled her down on the bed.

"Oh," she moaned.

"Sorry...but what were you saying?"

"Your hands..." She hesitated again.

"What's in my hands?" he said wearily. "Are there thorns in them?"

"Why do you ask these ridiculous questions? There's nothing in your hands...maybe there's nothing for me."

"What do you mean?"

"You...when you touch me...it seems as if you're under duress... you're forcing yourself."

"What rubbish is this?"

"Majid, it's no use...Majju...this drama should end now." A strange kind of cruelty flashed across her face. "This relationship cannot be forced, it must come from the heart."

"In other words, I'm under duress when I touch you...what are you talking about?"

"Yes…and the reason is very clear…it's obvious. We have both made a mistake."

"Mistake?"

"Look…Majju, try to understand. If an electric wire is snipped and attached to another wire, the current stops going through…and if…the wire is cut from the other side, the fuse goes off and one receives a terrible shock."

"Severed wires can be joined together again."

"That cannot be achieved by our coming together."

"What do you mean?"

"When wires are severed between husband and wife, it's the children who become the solution that keeps them together."

"Uff! You'll drive me mad. Abida, my love, I'm yours, my heart is yours."

"But your body is not mine."

"Abida…please."

"And no marriage can survive a division. These two parts of you are no good for anyone. The body that doesn't have a heart and that heart…"

"Abida…"

"I've thought a lot about this…thought so much that I'm exhausted. There's no other alternative. You can't live by dividing yourself. For this reason you will have to become whole again."

"You're confusing me. All right, let's say I accept your theory. Still, my heart and mind are yours and my body has worshipped you for years. If it strayed for a moment because of a tiny lapse, you won't accept it back to lie at your feet?"

"Don't insult the body like this. I need your body in my arms, not at my feet, but I know this better than you do. Your body is slave to your mind and I'm not in favour of actions that are forced."

"And my mind is slave to my body."

"Every man's mind is overpowered by his body. That's nothing to be ashamed of. It's the result of centuries of training. And it's better to come to terms with this rather than to keep feeling guilty all the time."

"In other words if my body is ready to wallow in filth I should also throw my mind into the gutter."

"It's not fair to weigh a person on the scales of intelligence and education. For example, Mona is a better woman than me. The assets she has…I don't have. For this reason filth is sometimes more desirable than sandalwood."

"What are you saying? You're blinded by a sense of inferiority."

"I'm right, otherwise she wouldn't have been able to lure you away like that."

"That's rubbish. No one lured me."

"Not your whole being, but she skimmed off the cream." Abida laughed hysterically. Her eyes had an odd glint in them. Her face was flushed. The tips of her fingers had turned icy and her palms were wet with perspiration. This cruel combination of fire and water had caused a kind of hysteria in her.

"So what is your advice?" Majid asked bitterly.

"You should marry her… Look…look…listen to me with a cool head. If you sat on hot coals and said that her body is not beautiful, I wouldn't believe you even then."

"There are thousands of women in the world whose bodies are more interesting than hers. That doesn't mean that I can shut out all common sense and continue to exist. You don't have any right to issue this royal decree. Just think for a minute how cruelly you're rejecting me. If that's how it was going to be, why didn't you make a decision when…"

"When a woman's ego comes forward and confronts her, that's when my thinking became clouded. I thought I had a right over you and this prevented me from realising that I couldn't win you back, that I wouldn't have you whole.

"Finding you incomplete, I have understood that it was my selfishness and meanness that made me agree that you should be split in two. I was really selfish then and I thought that losing you would be a blot on my womanliness, people might reproach you but at the same time they would pity me. Uff Allah! How could I allow the world to pity me? A false and stupid arrogance. The loser uses the worst kind of weapons. I was confident that I could flip a coin that had landed on the wrong side, that you would still be mine, and by being mother to your daughter I would in some way compensate for the injustice I had caused by being infertile."

"So, basically, you are trying to atone by flogging yourself."

"It's possible. Why not? Physical flogging is better than the blows suffered by one's conscience."

"So you've decided that in order to save yourself from the blows of your conscience and for your peace of mind, you will sacrifice me."

"Not happily. I've made these preparations after a great deal of analysis and thought."

"So now you're fully prepared to give me up."

Abida fell silent, seemed to be lost in thought.

"Is there no other way? Is there no place left in your heart for me?"

"It's the opposite. There is no place for anyone except you in my heart, nor for any other thought except that of you. For the last one and a half years it has been just you all around me. I've hated you, loved you, been angry with you, felt sympathy for you, just you. The links of every thought in my head reach back to you. And you say there's no place left in my heart for you! If I had devoted so much thought to God I would definitely have become a prophet by now. But inspite of all this I couldn't make you mine."

"You couldn't make me yours because you had never lost me in the first place. All right, you say there's anger in your heart for me, and love. This means I still live in your heart. So how can you decide to bury what is alive? Abida, my love…does your body not yearn for me?"

"Not yearn for you! My body aches for your touch."

"So then, when I touch you…"

"I… I don't know what happens. Perhaps my body becomes paralysed by my feelings of inadequacy!"

"Abida!" Majid was tormented by the strange look in Abida's eyes. "Come to me, come here…"

She was standing at the window, her back to him.

"Sometimes I think that if I had been strong everything would have been all right." She was talking to herself. "If I had died then…"

"Abida!"

"Everything would be fine."

"I couldn't have lived without you."

"You would have said this and would have wanted to kill yourself, but everyone would have comforted you by saying that nobody dies along with those who are dead, and eventually you would have come to understand. If I had died then you wouldn't have been forced to split your life into two, and you would be truly alive. You, your wife and your daughter."

"For God sake, stop this nonsense. What is wrong with you?"

She sounded remorseful again. "And it wouldn't be surprising if Mona were grateful that I had given her a chance to improve her life. And perhaps she would have called her Sabiha instead of Kitty."

Majid's head was spinning and brightly coloured spots danced in front of his eyes.

"When I first discovered this I went to the ocean with the intention of killing myself but I lost courage. My foot slipped on the sand and I fell into the water and splashed about, and my mouth was filled with sand and water and that's why... I was terrified. Not of death but of having to go through the stages of dying."

God knows what she was looking for outside the window. Perhaps the reflection of dreams that had been shattered. There was an expression of extreme weariness on her face. Overcome, Majid closed his eyes and fell back on the pillows.

~

Her dupatta fluttered like a pink butterfly, she slipped from his vision and was falling into a distant abyss.

"Abida!" he called from the depths of his being, but no sound emerged. Startled, he opened his eyes. Abida's body was draped over the windowsill.

"Abida!" His body shuddered once but in the next instant he had seized her in his arms.

"What's the matter, Majju?" She was frightened by the wild look in his eyes.

"You…you…from this window…"

"From the window…"

His brow was covered in perspiration.

"Oh, you thought I was going to jump out of the window and kill myself!"

"Yes. I was scared to death, Abida…you…"

Once again the suppleness of her body turned into steely rigidity.

"But this window is not even three feet from the ground! There's no chance even of a twisted ankle if I fall from here," she said laughing.

Poisonous thorns dug into Majid's hands.

"And if this window had been at a height of thirty feet instead of three?"

"Oh, my God! Then you would have pushed me down." Abida spoke affectionately.

"Abida."

"And people would have thought I was heartbroken and had committed suicide." A smile played upon her lips.

"You…you think that…" There was no remonstration in his voice, only a deep weariness.

"I don't want to think this Majid, but I've lost." She laughed. "You're well, now…why am I hanging around here to cause you distress?" Her voice was filled with tenderness.

He stared at her, heavy-eyed, silent.

"Hamida is going to stop here on her way to Nairobi. I'll write and tell her that Ammi Jaan needs me. She'll be here a month earlier. Her presence will liven up the place."

He remained silent.

"And then you can go and visit Ameena Khala for a few days in Bangalore."

"And then?"

"Ammi Jaan is very uncomfortable during the rainy season."

"Do you want to go?"

"The house needs repairs. I'm thinking that if Barre Abba's

house can be sold, then Shankar's and the doctor's loan can also be paid off."

"Give me an answer first. Do you want to go?"

"I…I think that…"

"Why?"

She silently straightened the creases in her shirt.

"Are you afraid? Like heroines in American films, you think I will kill you and…"

"I'm not afraid of dying… I… Majid… I'm beginning to distrust my mental state. My nerves are very…very…oh, how can I explain that I don't feel anything?"

"Are you beginning to distrust your mental state or me?"

"Both things are related, Majju, my love. The period we are going through is very critical."

"Yes, I know. What you are going through no woman has ever endured." Majid's face was flushed.

"I can't say anything about that, but perhaps I'm not perfect like other women. I am not generous in spirit, I hold grudges."

"Abida, I have admitted my crime, I have asked for forgiveness."

Abida wearily picked up the glass on the table nearby and dropped it. Glass shards scattered on the floor like a scream.

"If I now admit my mistake will these shards become whole again?"

"So you want to go. Whether the shards become whole or are thrown in the garbage."

"Time heals all wounds. Perhaps because of your illness some scabs came off."

"Abida, do you know what I used to think once?"

"What?"

"That if you were ever unfaithful I would strangle you and then shoot myself, but now…"

"But now…"

"Now I pray that you falter and betray me, then the scales would be balanced. That you would be as sinful as me, then this distance between us would be obliterated."

"That's why I say we shouldn't be together, because something terrible that shouldn't happen might happen." She was suddenly out of breath, as if she had run a great distance.

"Tell Hamida to bring my warm clothes, it will be chilly in Bangalore." Majid turned on his side to face the wall.

Abida quickly started counting plates and cutlery and began putting them away in cupboards. Whatever extra linen there was she packed with her own things. Who knows how long she would be away. People are not to be trusted; even the brooms will be stolen.

Abida always wore hand-dyed crinkled dupattas. The ones with trimmings that her in-laws had given her lasted a whole year. When the colours faded she would dye them herself and make them last a while longer. But of late she had only been using white dupattas. And then one day she took off her gold bangles saying they bothered her. Majid observed all this quietly and his heart sank. He wasn't dead yet, why was Abida mourning him already?

"Where's your ring?" The ring his mother had given him to present to Abida on their wedding night.

"Which ring? Oh…the stone was loose, I gave it to Shankar to get it repaired."

"What ring? Bhabi didn't give me any ring." Shankar was baffled when Majid asked him.

"Oh…she must have forgotten." But asking Abida for a clarification was an insult to his ego.

He came across the empty frame that had once held their wedding picture lying on a shelf in the almirah; it had always been on the dressing-table. He quietly put it back. He found shredded fragments of that part of the photograph containing Abida's picture in the waste-basket. His own picture had disappeared.

This time Abida was severing all her connections before she left.

Then one day the plates and cutlery were laid out once again on the sideboard. Towels and blankets came out of the large trunk. And the polishers for the copper pots were summoned from Shankar's house.

But the rings and bangles didn't return.

Abida swooped like an eagle when the mail arrived. Leaving

Majid's correspondence on his desk, she immediately shut herself in the bathroom. One day he saw fragments of a fancy envelope on which the address had been typed very stylishly, floating in the toilet. Abida would emerge from the bathroom looking distracted and then he would hear her opening and closing the locker in the Godrej almirah.

"I'll be back in a minute, just going down to the corner."

Majid was becoming an expert at espionage. She wasn't going down to the corner, she was going further, to the post office.

"Perhaps she's planning to work," Majid told himself. The pain in his hands and feet had returned. He had taken time off from work, without pay. Abida's mother had sent them a draft for two thousand that seemed to have grown like wild flowers. He always handed over every penny of his salary to Abida. He had sent in a request for his full salary for leave due, but only half had been approved.

"Did you get a letter from Hamida?" he finally asked after being patient for ten or twelve days.

"No."

"Why?"

Instead of giving him an answer she went into the next room and began to discuss the different colour schemes for various rooms.

"What did I ask you?" Majid called out as she passed through the drawing room.

"What?" she asked archly. "I don't know."

"What do you mean?"

"Look, stop bothering me. The painter says lilac won't be suitable for the bedroom."

"Lilac?"

"The colour, light purple."

"What is this craziness?"

"All right, if not lilac, then let's go for light beige." She completely ignored Majid and continued arguing with the painter.

For some reason Majid was overcome by a sense of relief. He was reminded of his bride of twelve years ago. She would wake up startled from deep sleep and say, "Light brown curtains in every room would be fine, but the divan should definitely have a brown cover."

And he would make fun of her domestic preoccupations.

"Do you think I should take a course in interior decoration?" she would ask eagerly.

"Oh, no."

"Then cooking lessons maybe? I'm wasting my time doing nothing all day."

"Nonsense."

"So which course would be suitable in your opinion?"

"Intercourse!" he would grab her and say teasingly.

"Please..." she would blush and turn her face away. "Always thinking of dirty things."

"You're referring to the most beautiful thing in life as a dirty thing."

He drew a deep breath. Would Abida's dreams ever be revived again?

"All right, what were you asking? This painter is such a nuisance, always shirking." She came and plonked herself on the chair next to his bed.

"Did you get a reply from Hamida?" He didn't really want to know.

"No, I didn't write to her so why would I get a reply? Oh, my God, that's terrible!"

"What's happened?"

"I must be going mad. Well, I'll have it dyed."

"What is all this nonsense?" Majid was irritated now.

"The bedroom curtains are pink, so I think dark beige will look better, or pistachio green." She seemed to be talking to herself, as if Majid was not in the room with her.

"For God's sake!" said Majid, exasperated.

She began laughing and laughed so much that tears ran from her eyes. Then she looked at him fondly. "Why don't you just ask if I'm going or not."

A cotton ball seemed to have got stuck in Majid's throat. "Tell me..."

"What?" She had decided to be playful.

"Are you going?" Majid asked, his heart racing.

"Naa..."

"Why not?" he asked in a stifled voice. Was he hearing her right?

"Because that's what I want."

"And…the shards of glass?"

"I've thrown them in the garbage."

He kept looking at her through half-shut eyes.

And what about the torn fragments of the envelope, the trips to the post office, closing of the latch on the locker?

His head was exploding. Someone was pumping his heart from below. Whirlwinds of dry sand began to dance in his lungs.

He extended his arms. Abida's dupatta slipped from her shoulders like an onion peel.

~

The bihishti's wife was wiping his eyes with her smelly, dirty dupatta, but the tears in his eyes had dried up. Sweat was trickling down and being absorbed by the dirt floor of the small room where firewood was stored. She was laughing at his inexperience.

But Abida didn't laugh.

Outside a light rain was falling. Crumpled like a heap of cloth, Majid was sobbing. His eyelids were sore from Abida's starched dupatta.

Just as a muddied dawn was breaking the two of them fell into tormented sleep.

"Where is your jewellery?" Majid asked her one day.

"I left it with Ammi Jaan." Abida was changing a cushion cover.

"Not that, what you wear all the time. Your earrings."

"I have them."

"And the bangles, the ring?"

"I have them all. Why do you ask?"

"Why don't you wear them?"

"They bother me. But I'll wear them if you want me to."

"Wear them now."

"Why? Don't I look nice without jewellery?"

"You don't trust me any more."

"There you go being silly again. By God's grace, you're the father of a daughter now, how can anyone not trust you?"

"Abida."

"Hmm."

"Divorce me."

"Why? Is the worm crawling in your head again?"

"You asked for a divorce once and I refused. Now I think I'm dead."

"Majju darling, I asked Veenaji. She said this happens after what you went through. Everything will be all right."

"And what if it isn't?"

"Majju, marriage is not just one kind of emotion. The bazaar is open to satisfy the emotion you're talking about. I have no complaints. But if you think that this is all a hoax, that I'm…that I'm the reason for your pain, then how can anyone stop you from letting another woman bring you back to life?"

"No one can bring me back to life, not a second woman, or a third or fourth—I don't need a woman."

"Then do something for me."

"What?"

"Don't think of me as a woman, think of me as a friend, a companion, anything you want. I'm also related to you, so think of me as a relative."

"You're impossible."

"No doubt. Now stop this nonsense."

"Abida," Majid asked after closing his eyes for a few minutes.

"Yes, my love."

"I don't think this job is going to last much longer."

"Well, you can still take ten more months of leave."

"Without pay."

"Well, we'll die of starvation then."

"You'll die of starvation."

"Well, I died once for you, now starvation will kill us both. Anyway, you took care of me for twelve years, now it's time for me to take care of you."

"You're impossible."

"Is there any doubt about that?"

"But adorably impossible."

"Which is why I'm not getting a divorce."

"You've turned me into a cripple."

"So you won't run away!" She laughed lightly.

"Abida."

"Uff-oh! What more do you want to say?"

"Stop wearing this pink dupatta."

"Here, I'll take it off." She removed the dupatta and threw it at him. Majid shot up and pulled her down onto the cushions.

The bell rang with the sound of paper falling into the mailbox. Abida tore herself from his embrace. Picking up the dupatta that lay like a pink onion peel on the floor she ran towards the door.

She returned with the letters, put them in front of him and walked to the kitchen.

"Forgot to give instructions about the soup."

But Majid knew she was lying, that she was hiding something.

He concluded that the answer to his dilemma lay in the locker of Abida's Godrej almirah. She wouldn't leave the key lying around even for a minute and Majid didn't have the courage to ask for it.

But if he didn't open the locker he would go mad. For several days he had been wondering how he could get to it without creating suspicions. Abida would be walking around the house, keys swinging from her hand and Majid would feel he was losing his sanity. What was she hiding there?

One day, fate came to his aid and he saw that the bunch of keys was peeping from under the pillow like a mischievous lover. He lay down on the pretext of feeling unwell. Unaware of his sneaky plans Abida sat in front of the mirror combing her hair. Perhaps she was planning to go to the post office, which is why she was wearing a sari. After getting ready she went up to the door, then feeling the absence of the silver key-ring on her waist she turned around.

Majid felt life ebbing from him. He pretended not to notice. For a while she stood near the pillow, pondering over whether to remove the keys from under it. Majid's heart was pounding so violently he was sure she could hear it.

After she left he remained still for a few minutes. When the sound of Abida's footsteps receded he got up, his body shaking. He didn't even know which key opened which lock. His body was racked with shadow pains, his left arm felt inert, and there was a heaviness in his shoulder. This could be a heart attack but he was putting his life on the line, trying desperately to fit one key after another into the lock. Finally, the cupboard opened. There was nothing in the locker. A few artificial gold bangles studded with stones in one corner, some pieces of cosmetic jewellery, a cheque book and electricity bills.

He staggered back when he saw a thick file in the other corner. How heavy it was for an ordinary file. He picked it up and walked over to the chair with great difficulty.

It wasn't a file. It was a record of Majid's misdeeds. Every single letter from Mona had been filed neatly and in order in it. In addition, every single penny that had been spent on her had been accounted for. Hospital expenses, tips to the nurses, taxi fares, the cost of their stay in Poona, details about the money spent on clothes for Kitty, on yarn, on knitting needles. Three hundred rupees a month had been agreed upon, but in every column there was an addition of another fifty to a hundred. But the receipt for the last amount that had been received a few days ago was for five hundred rupees. He had never imagined that a minor indiscretion would have such serious consequences. People committed heinous crimes, indulged in adulterous pleasures, and just walked away at the end of them. In the old days an adulterer was stoned, but the tiny stones that rained continuously on him had turned into a mountain. And yet he was still breathing.

Mona's most recent letter differed from her earlier ones. The paper was beautiful, smooth and fragrant. The address was also not that of Duncan Road, it was Omar Park. In this latest letter she had written that because of her increased workload she urgently needed an ayah. She had a woman from Mangalore to do the baby's work, but she wouldn't wash her diapers, so a maid had to be hired. The rent for the flat alone was three hundred and forty, but she couldn't burden Saran with the baby's…

A spear sank into Majid's shoulder. Needles seemed to be pricking his brain.

In the end she had written that if things continued to be so difficult she might have to send the baby to an orphanage; the receipt for the five hundred that Abida had sent her to take care of the situation was secured neatly to the letter.

"So now you've started stealing as well!" Abida snatched the file from his hands. Majid hadn't heard her coming in.

"By 'as well' you mean along with my depravity…"

"All right, please stop talking like this." She let go of the file and turned guiltily to the almirah.

"How did letters addressed to me get to you?"

Her back to him, she continued rummaging through the locker casually.

"Answer me," he roared.

"Shankar sent them to me."

"The bastard! Why did he forward my letters to you?"

"It's not his fault. I asked him to."

"Why?"

"Because you had entrusted the matter to me."

"Is that why you dash off to the post office every chance you get?"

"I don't dash off at all, I walk very slowly. I swear to God." She closed the almirah and turned to smile at him.

"Another five hundred after the first three hundred. Who gave you permission to send it?"

"I gave myself permission."

"She kept blackmailing you, and you? You didn't think it was necessary to mention any of this to me."

"It would just have distressed you further. You need a lot of rest after this illness."

"You didn't think that when I found out about it, I would…"

"I thought you would never find out. After you handed the matter over to me you never asked about it. You never enquired about anything. I was sure you would never find this file, and I never imagined in my wildest dreams that you would become suspicious and start searching through my almirah."

She ran her hand, which was dry as paper, over his forehead. Incensed by her touch Majid became even angrier.

"There's a limit to everything." He pushed her hand away. "I admire the hard work you've put into preparing a list of my crimes."

"List of crimes." Abida's colour drained. She quickly began straightening out the wrinkles in her dupatta.

"Afraid that I might forget and renege, you have."

"No, no, Majju, I swear on your life… I have… I…" The muscles of her face quivered. "I didn't want to keep reminding you, but I never thought you didn't love your offspring, or that you don't have a relationship with the child's mother. Your relationship with me will last as long as we are alive, but your relationship with your daughter, then with her children and their children, that will stretch on and on."

"Your generosity is admirable. You're a goddess, a goddess. Let me worship at your feet." Majid aimed an arrow at her dramatically.

"You can say even crueller things if you want."

"And you will tolerate them so that the burden of remorse weighing heavily on my chest becomes heavier."

"Keep saying what you want, spew out all the poison. Actually, I should be weeping and whining and creating a commotion since that's the way decent women are expected to behave. But when you shared your secret with me you thought of me as your friend, not your wife. You did something unusual, I responded in an unusual way. You know how organised I am. I don't do anything haphazardly. This file is not a list of your crimes. Anyway, let me throw this damn file into the fire. Satisfied?"

"Why did you suddenly change your mind about going away?"

"Majju, after having spent twelve years with you I've got used to you. I consider your burden mine, your illness is mine, if you eat properly I feel full, if you have pain in your joints, my heart aches. I still don't believe that there's no place for me in your heart. Yes, go ahead and say I'm insufferable, I'm old fashioned, I'm one of those women who worships their husbands. So tell me, what will you do if I regard you as mine even after we're divorced?"

"For God's sake, don't put me on such a high pedestal, I feel as if I'm suffocating. I won't be able to tolerate such a great burden." His face became distorted.

"Oh God, Majid...my love." Abida began cracking her knuckles nervously.

"This is not love, this is suffocation. If I touch you the blood in your veins seems to freeze... I'm terrified of this kind of love. Only corpses love like this. I'm repelled by this dead body." He began to pace restlessly. Then suddenly he grasped both her hands in his and said, "Don't drown in the well that I have dug, Abida, escape from this spider's web."

"How can I escape? Is there a way out?" She covered her face with both hands and sighed.

"I will arrange for a ticket right away." He got up.

"The time to leave has come and gone."

"What do you mean?"

"If I hadn't listened to you and had left in the very beginning, everything would have been fine. But I couldn't go. My selfishness and weakness placed chains upon my feet."

"I stopped you."

"But why did I stay? Because I wanted to."

"Your reasoning will drive me mad."

"Her life was destroyed because of me. She had to turn to Saranji for help because the doors of this house are closed to her. The rights are all in my name. I'm Mrs. Majid, and even though she is the mother of your daughter she has no legal status. This is not law, it's a joke."

"If someone vomits in a filthy drain and maggots begin to crawl in it, will one marry the drain?"

"You think you're doing me a favour by calling Mona a drain and the child a maggot, but I'm not such a shallow person. I've seen Mona more intimately than you have. Yes, yes, you slept with her, but we've spent many grief-stricken and hopeless nights together, and together mourned your infidelity. Do you know, she used to feel great pity for me. She didn't believe for a second that you were abandoning her because of a dull, uninteresting person like me. She thought you were fickle by nature and that I would cover up your depraved deeds for the rest of my life because this is a barren woman's duty."

"You joined hands with a prostitute and created a front against me."

"How could we miserable women fight you? We were wringing each other's necks behind your back. Sometimes you kick and sometimes you rub your nose in the dirt to get your way. All right, I'm ready to get a divorce from you on the condition that you marry her. Do you agree?"

"The same stubborn arguments! I've told you before, there's nothing in common between us."

"Because she has been used by other men besides you? Then admit that we have nothing in common either, because you too have been used by others but I have always been devoted to you alone. Yes, go ahead and say that I'm arguing for the sake of arguing, but this ploy won't work."

"You're being irrational. Pleading her cause is a waste of time."

"Majid Sahib, have you ever thought…when Kitty grows up… what kind of decisions will she make about herself? After Mona's lovers have dispersed one by one, won't she lead her daughter down the same path? I'm comfortably settled in my house—won't my conscience trouble me? After Saran…"

"There's no question of 'after Saran' yet! He'll live for another forty years at least. He's healthy and in very good shape."

"Well, the fact that he is in very good physical shape is the problem. He can mourn and move on easily. Saran changes his car every six months. There's no need for him to take a break between women. As I was coming out of the post office yesterday I saw him leaving Grand Bazaar in the company of a beautiful young woman, both of them carrying packages. They looked very nervous when they saw me. He said she was the daughter of one of his friends, in Bombay for a visit. She is staying in Saran's executive suite at the Taj."

"And where did you get this last bit of information?"

"I got it from where I should have got it." She smiled a little secret smile.

"One won't find many wives who are generous enough to be taking such good care of their husband's girlfriend's lovers." The bitterness in Majid's tone became venomous. Abida could only stare at him with a wounded look. Every move she was making seemed to backfire.

"My love, you're very tired. Rest for a while." She tried to give him her hand him but he turned away from her loving gesture. There was a storm raging inside his head, his ears reverberated with a constant buzzing. He placed his head on the pillow like a defeated player and closed his eyes.

~

Majid closed the door behind him and entered the drawing room through the dimly-lit passage. Abida was standing on a stool, lovingly cleaning the imaginary dust from Ammi Jaan's picture with a corner of her pink dupatta. She craned her neck to see Majid but the words froze on her tongue. Their eyes met and locked.

"Mmm…Majjan…" She stepped down from the stool.

Seeing Majid stumble as if he were drunk, she reached towards him like a fluttering butterfly but didn't have the courage to touch him. Majid's body was taut like an arrow strung on the bow and his eyes were burning.

"Here you are," she said as if from a great distance.

"Yes," Majid replied from even further away.

"Why did you leave the house when you were so tired?" Abida asked reproachfully. "Come, sit down." She brought his special chair forward but he kept looking through her.

"Shall I ask for tea?" She turned to go to the kitchen. The look in Majid's eyes terrified her. When she returned with the tea-tray she found Majid standing where she had left him. His hands hung helplessly by his sides as if they had forgotten what their function was. Abida put the tray on the table. Then she sat down on the carpet.

"What did she say?" She spoke abruptly.

"She said she would decide after talking to you."

"Oh." She put two teaspoons of sugar in the cup. Picking up the teapot with a corner of her dupatta, she started pouring. "You wouldn't have missed the train if you had waited till Sunday. Why did you go to her? Why did you have to beg before a base woman like her?"

"Well, you're an expert in fixing things that go wrong. When the matter is entrusted to you, it will automatically be resolved."

"That ungrateful woman! How dare she treat you with such disrespect." Abida felt her blood boil.

"Just the opposite! She's buried under the weight of your kindness and cannot take a single step without your consent."

Abida was at a loss for words.

"I don't know if I put sugar in your tea or not." She touched the sugar pot with shaking hands.

"Every single pore of her being is trapped in the mesh of your benevolence and generosity. Your devotion has erased the black stains of my infidelity. I gave her unhappiness and disrespect. But you gave her a mother's love, a sister's sympathy and a friend's sincerity. You became the oar of her sinking boat and saved her from a life of perpetual uncertainty. You sent her money in my name, but she knows perfectly well that you sold your jewellery and…"

"Damn the wretched jewellery." She started stirring the tea rapidly.

"She's seen many lovers but this is the first time she's had to deal with a lover's beloved like you. She's extremely scared of you." Majid was smiling impishly but Abida's heart lurched when she saw that the look in his eyes reflected sarcasm not devotion.

"I…I…" she said nervously.

"If you want, my destiny can be reversed. If you order her to take pity on your beloved husband as a reward for all your kindnesses and your generosity, tell her that he will be destroyed and his unfortunate heart, which is actually your heart, will be shattered otherwise."

Placing his hand on his heart, Majid continued dramatically. "I am your beloved Majjan. I am yours, my heart, my brain, my kidneys and lungs, are all yours, the morsel in my mouth reaches your stomach, if I can't digest my food, you have to vomit, if my veins are slashed it is your blood that flows. You, you, you are all of me…and I'm just an illusion, a complete fantasy."

Abida's lips moved but no sound emerged. She was staring at him.

"If you put in a good word for me she will gather me in her embrace, I will have your permission to take her into my arms, and with your best wishes she and I will…"

"Majid…what are you saying?"

"You covered up my sin. I won't be able to deny your benevolence for many lifetimes." He was out of breath.

"Majid, you're exhausted…please." She seemed to be looking for something in her lap.

"I won't rest."

"Listen, Majid…"

"No, I don't have time to listen…it's your turn to listen today."

"Say what you want… I'm listening." She looked at her hands as she turned them upside down.

"Did you know where I had gone?"

"When you didn't get back from the office on time, I thought."

"And you knew what answer I would receive."

"I…I had…" she stammered.

"You know what's unknown. Why did you have to ask then?"

"I…well…Majid, you…" Her lap was empty. She felt as if she had stolen something.

"Because you believe in playing every single chess piece on the board."

"Allah!" There was nothing in her hands.

"And this was your last assault. You had been pushing me for several days. There's deception in a woman's temperament—I don't want to repeat this hackneyed sentiment nor do I believe it. But Abida, you were not honest with me."

"You're not in your senses, wait until you are feeling calmer, more peaceful…"

"Peace, peace, peace! I'm repelled by this word." The veins stood out on his forehead. "The time for peace has passed. I've barricaded all of the enemy's trenches. My resignation was accepted today."

"But you could have asked for more leave…"

"It seems that the time for my leave-taking is not that far." The congestion in his lungs meant he couldn't breathe properly.

"Majju, I beg you." She began sobbing loudly.

"Even if I wanted to live, I can't now." He stared wildly at the walls around him. "I can't become a puppet for someone's entertainment. You are probably praying to God that I should become a cripple so that you can be my hands and feet, become my tongue and serve me for the rest of your life."

"God forbid! I beg of you, Allah…" She was trembling from head to toe.

"And perhaps I never loved you. I saw you and I thought my life would be incomplete without you. This is not love, this is selfishness. I acquired you to make my life complete. And you…you heard stories about my waywardness and resolved to possess me. You were fond of domesticating wild pigeons, weren't you? Wild animals fed from your hands." Words became entangled with each other and fell one upon the other.

"Oh God… Oh God… I will die."

"No, you won't die, your heart will continue to beat in your chest, and after I'm gone my heart will also beat in your bosom… I…you have gathered my entire being into yours, now it…it will never be dispersed…never fall into an abyss. With the heights of your being it will soar higher, higher still…higher than my reach…my breath will sob on your lips, the light of my eyes will shine in yours." Nonsensical words began to fall from Majid's lips, his eyes bulged and his face became burnished like burnt copper. He began to scratch it with both hands.

And just as Abida was trying to hold him up, he fell face down.

The air around them stilled. As if Bombay's soul had been seized. Abida's ears were blocked. The darkness in the room thickened. She carefully brought Majid to the divan and straightened his body. With her cold hands she closed his wildly staring eyes, tied her pink dupatta around the jaws that kept dropping and meticulously positioned his hands by his sides. Pulling off the ribbon from her ponytail she bound his big toes together and then, like an obedient child, sat down on the stool.

For a moment there was a slight movement in Majid's half-open eyelids. He looked at Abida through the corners of his eyes, a smile quivered on his lips, a huge laugh became a storm in his chest...and then the world stood still.

Majid's last look told a story.

"How diligent you are, you've readied me even before I am dead. I hope that in your prayers you will have made arrangements for me to be comfortable in the next world too."

Weary with the weight of her bridal bangles, Abida's wrists slumped, and like a shooting star she found herself drowning in a void.

~

The doorbell rang again and again...all in her imagination.

She heard bells ringing for no reason. Perhaps the husbands in the flats next door were returning from work. Her doorbell would never ring again, no one would take her in his arms the moment the door opened, never kiss her dry lips again...never kiss her again... she was lying in a grave, there were people all the way to the top... tears were falling...thick clouds of grief descended, the world was full but her life was empty...her wrists were as light as flowers, her white unstarched dupatta was drenched in the terrible odour of camphor and frankincense.

The bell rang again, sounding like a sick child's whine. As if in some other world, a faraway world, she carefully rearranged her scattered dreams and locked them in the almirah, placed the half-knitted sweater in the drawer, pushed the slippers under the bed with her feet and picked up the socks and stuffed them in a corner.

When she got up and opened the door to make sure she was not dreaming, she saw Mona turning to leave. She came back when she heard the door open.

"I dozed off."

"Uff, your daughter is so heavy." She was out of breath.

"Don't say things like that. Give her to me," taking the girl from her.

"I won't take her back then!" She laughed a phony laugh.

"All right, that's enough. Where are you headed?" Abida sat down on the sofa with the child.

"It's the last race in Poona. After that we were planning to go to Mahabaleshwar for two days. But she will be a lot of work for you."

"Thanks for your sympathy...is Saran ji well?" she said to change the subject.

"He's well. His divorce will be final in October."

"Oh, well, congratulations."

"I'm... I'm so selfish. Whenever I need to I dump her on you. And now I don't know what to do."

"Don't worry, you'll begin to understand everything. Is the wedding before Christmas or..."

"No, there's no reason to delay it. There's no trusting men, who knows when they may have a change of heart. The iron's hot at this time, but I wonder if...if..."

Abida didn't finish her sentence for her. But her heart was beating violently. Whatever Mona had to say she would have to say without her help.

"Saran ji doesn't like children at all."

Abida remained silent.

"I've fought with him several times...but he's ready to pay."

"How much would this little thing need, and of course she's not a poor man's child."

"If I had given her to you then you would have taken her happily."

Abida said nothing.

"I didn't give her to you because I was stubborn. But I was never at peace. I always felt I had stolen someone else's baby."

Abida silently ran her little finger through Sabiha's hair.

"Have you noticed something? She looks more like you than me. There were times when I got really angry, used to think you were a magician, that you had begun stealing her from me from the time she was in my womb."

Abida said nothing, just sat quietly like someone who had committed a crime.

"But this was my foolishness. Actually, it was a family resemblance. Majid Sahib was your first cousin, wasn't he?"

Abida didn't answer her.

"Is it possible that one woman's child can grow in another woman's body?" Mona asked, half-afraid.

Abida's lips still didn't move.

"Nothing is beyond God's grace." Mona made the sign of the cross on her and left without looking back.

After she had gone, Abida picked up her sleeping daughter, draped her silky soft, somnolent arms around her own neck like a necklace, then tiptoed to her bedroom.

She gently put the girl down where Majid had once slept. She was overcome by drowsiness again and yawning, she settled into her own spot and fell into a deep slumber the minute her head touched the pillow.

She hadn't known such beautiful, intense and carefree sleep in years.

In Majid's picture hanging on the wall, his open eyes were inert, unmoving.

How could there be any sign of sleep in them?

www.ingramcontent.com/pod-product-compliance
Lightning Source LLC
Chambersburg PA
CBHW050742230626
47052CB00004BA/1049